ANDROMEDA

ANDROMEDA

Therese Bohman

Translated from the Swedish by
Marlaine Delargy

Other Press
New York

The cost of this translation was supported by a subsidy from
the Swedish Arts Council, gratefully acknowledged.

Production editor: Yvonne E. Cárdenas
Text designer: Patrice Sheridan
This book was set in Times New Roman and Brandon Grotesque
by Alpha Design & Composition of Pittsfield, NH

1 3 5 7 9 10 8 6 4 2

Library of Congress Cataloging-in-Publication Data
Names: Bohman, Therese, 1978- author. | Delargy, Marlaine, translator.
Title: Andromeda : a novel / Therese Bohman ; translated from the Swedish
by Marlaine Delargy.
Other titles: Andromeda. English
Description: New York : Other Press, 2025.
Identifiers: LCCN 2024019120 (print) | LCCN 2024019121 (ebook) |
ISBN 9781635424188 (paperback) | ISBN 9781635424195 (ebook)
Subjects: LCGFT: Novels.
Classification: LCC PT9877.12.O48 A5513 2025 (print) |
LCC PT9877.12.O48 (ebook) | DDC 839.73/8—dc23/eng/20240503
LC record available at https://lccn.loc.gov/2024019120
LC ebook record available at https://lccn.loc.gov/2024019121

Wohin gehen wir? Immer nach Hause.

—NOVALIS

1.

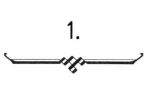

THE PUBLISHING HOUSE looks like a ship moored in the city center, a large, pale building crowned with a roof terrace. The facade is a grid of wood and granite, and flags flutter in the wind, adorned with an ornate but resolute *R*. *R* for Rydéns.

It is on the roof terrace that the parties are held. Standing up there you feel as if you own the entire city, as if everything is lying at your feet. Slowly you are enveloped by the twilight, which creeps closer and closer as the hum of conversation grows louder and the countless fairy lights begin to glow. Young men in white shirts and black waistcoats stand behind the bar, they pour a glass of chilled white wine and place the glass on a small paper coaster bearing the same *R* as on the flags: gold leaf against a cream-colored background. It is said that one such coaster was found among Strindberg's effects after his death.

The autumn party marks the real beginning of the publishing year. Anticipation fills the air, like at the start of a new school semester, and this season's authors mingle nervously, with the hopes of the finance department weighing heavily on their shoulders.

But the spring parties are the best, those are the ones that are legendary. You stand in the endless May evening, watching the dusk slowly descend over rooftops and church spires, and everything feels like a game. It doesn't matter if we employees have a little too much to drink, because on this occasion we don't have to be representative and professional, we are allowed to celebrate the year that has passed, the prizes and nominations that were acknowledged only with the obligatory cake at coffee time in December because everyone was so stressed in the run-up to Christmas, the spring debuts that have gone better than we dared hope. We forget that several weeks of hard work lie ahead, with everything that has to go to print before midsummer, the final edits, the blurbs for all those back covers, the proofs, the manuscripts you fall asleep over and eventually almost know by heart, those that will generate fresh acclaim and nominations in the autumn. We help ourselves to another glass beneath the vast lavender-colored sky.

I had heard about the parties long before I started at Rydéns.

It was the spring term of 2009, a ten-week internship, and I was happy and proud to be one of the few who had secured a position with a major publisher. At the same time, I had never felt so inexperienced. The only job I'd had up to that point was as a temporary home aide and maid, I knew almost nothing about what went on in a publishing house. I had to learn every detail from scratch: what to wear, how to use the printer and the photocopier, how to integrate with colleagues, making sure to refer to them as colleagues and not coworkers or workmates. And how to navigate around the hierarchies that clearly exist, while at the same time being expected to take every opportunity to show my independence and impressive initiative.

During the first few weeks I often cried when I got home in the evenings, clutching my bundle of manuscripts.

I had just moved from student housing on Lappkärrsberget to a one-bedroom sublet in Skanstull, and I hadn't expected to feel so lonely. When I tried to contemplate my life from the outside, it almost came across as a clichéd image of alienation in a big city—being so close to other people, yet so far away from them. I was an insignificant human being among thousands of others, one of those who dashed across Ringvägen before the light changed, who hurried down the stairs to the subway platform, pushed my way onto the first train heading north, and got off at Hötorget.

I had a nagging sense that something was missing, a low-intensity perception of insufficiency that was hard to put into words. My social circle was built entirely on chance and temporary circumstances, and would probably disappear when my studies were over. I spent most evenings at home reading, embedded in a feeling of slight listlessness. Sometimes I went for a walk down by Årstaviken, following the quayside to Danvikstull, then standing there gazing at the warmly glowing windows in Hammarby Sjöstad.

I often felt as if nothing in my life were real, or at least not as real as in the lives of my acquaintances. Somehow they seemed more rooted in the world, sure of what they wanted from their future and what they needed to do in order to achieve it. At the same time, that feeling was frustrating because, after all, I had something I could only have dreamed of a few years ago: a place to live in central Stockholm, a university education that was nearing completion, an internship with a major publishing house. Apart from the poor finances that go with being a student, and the fact that the spring was late this year, I didn't have much to complain about.

I hardly dared open my mouth during meetings at Rydéns. Everyone else seemed so confident, defending their opinions in a polished and professional way, or taking a relaxed, almost nonchalant approach. They radiated established practice and self-assurance, neither of which I possessed. I often thought that I must say something, otherwise they would think I wasn't interested, when in fact I wanted nothing more than to make some smart comment. But I just couldn't come up with anything smart enough. Eventually it became a kind of obsession: so many meetings and still I had hardly said a word. If I were to speak, I imagined the others looking up, staring at me, and thinking, "Wow, she can actually talk!"

One day there were reviews of one of Rydéns's recently published novels in almost every daily newspaper. The reception was almost universally lukewarm, just as I had expected. In fact I didn't really understand why it had been published at all. That same afternoon I happened to find myself at the coffee machine in the lunchroom with Gunnar, the company's editor in chief.

"Not very good reviews," he said to make conversation, nodding in the direction of the culture sections of the morning papers that lay open on the table.

"To be honest, I didn't think much of the book myself," I said tentatively. This was perfectly true, but I still regretted my words as soon as I had spoken. They came across as far more critical than I had intended.

"Oh?" Gunnar replied. "Why not?"

There was no aggression in his question, no hint of wounded pride. He sounded genuinely curious.

"I just thought it was too contrived. There's no real pain or emotion. It feels dishonest."

"Harsh," Gunnar said quietly.

For a moment I thought I had made a fool of myself, broken some kind of loyalty code which decreed that you must never criticize anything published by your own company. Had I ruined my chances of staying on at Rydéns after my internship?

But then he smiled at me.

"I agree. I said exactly the same thing when Jenny presented it back in the autumn, but sometimes you just have to give in. Come with me."

He led the way along the corridor to his office, where he handed me three manuscripts with rubber bands around them.

"Read these and see if they're worth pursuing," he said.

"Okay…?"

"They're by first-time authors. They've been through an initial reading, but that doesn't necessarily mean much. We'll catch up on Friday morning."

"Okay," I said again.

It was incredibly difficult. I tried to guess what the correct opinion of the manuscripts might be, but I felt exactly like I did during the meetings at Rydéns, and during university seminars where I never knew what I was supposed to say about the texts we'd read and always wondered how it was that everyone else had so much to contribute. Where did they get it all from? I wasn't used to expressing my views. Even though our tutors constantly stressed the importance of independent analysis and reflection, no one ever taught us these skills.

Now I didn't even have a group to hide behind, someone else's opinion to ride on. I read through all three manuscripts quickly, hoping that I would have an intuitive feeling for what was bad and what was good, but my brain kept forestalling me, making me doubt my own instincts. Two of the manuscripts had a clear message, and I could already picture the blurb on the back cover, empathetic phrases about highly relevant contemporary depictions giving an important perspective. I knew everyone would be on board with that description, and the novels would be regarded as both good and significant literary texts. The third manuscript was completely different: enigmatic, idiosyncratic, poetic. Compared with the other two it was unworldly, harder to explain and therefore harder to sell. My gut told me that it was the best, but I wasn't sure how to justify my view. I was also reluctant to bear the responsibility for rejecting manuscripts that might be successfully launched by another publisher.

I became increasingly despondent as the week went on. Soon it was Thursday evening, and my computer pinged, alerting me to the group chat where a few of my fellow students had decided to go out for a drink. I left my manuscripts and went to meet them. I'd decided that I might as well give up and tell the truth when I met with Gunnar the next day: I don't know what I think. This is too difficult for me. I guess the world of publishing isn't my thing after all.

I had several drinks, quickly and carelessly, because I might as well get drunk now that I'd failed at my internship and lacked instinct and opinions and personality. I sat in silence on the uncomfortable seat and listened to my classmates having a boring discussion about some book on the syllabus. They sounded so infuriatingly smug, as if they were in a seminar at the university rather than three beers down among friends, they spoke as if they were trying to impress someone, yet at the same time they weren't really saying anything, or at least nothing that meant anything.

Suddenly everything became clear to me.

I excused myself and hurried home, anxious not to lose my anger. I thought the subway was unusually slow and that the traffic lights on Ringvägen took an extra-long time to change to green. When I got back I spread out the three manuscripts in front of me, and as I quickly leafed through them again it seemed perfectly obvious: The third manuscript was the only one that was any good. It was the only one that counted as literature in the way I thought literature should be: strong-willed, courageous, written with a clear aesthetic vision.

The other two were as meaningless as my classmates' pretentious nonsense, written in impeccable but dull prose, lying heavy and dead on every single page. The subject matter might have been convincing on paper, but they were both irredeemably boring. It was as if the authors had followed a template for significant depictions of contemporary society, which made reading them entirely pointless because you knew from the get-go what they were trying to do. Why would I want to publish something like that? Why would I recommend something that I despised? It was in fact the manuscript that at first glance had appeared to be the least relevant that was the best: It had a genuine purpose.

That's exactly what I said to Gunnar when he called me into his office the following morning. I felt really important, sitting there in a 1960s leather armchair that was probably part of the building's original decor, surrounded by his untidy bookshelves and the patchwork of paintings on the walls.

"These," I began, pointing to the two manuscripts I didn't like, "read as if they've been written according to a template for contemporary Swedish literature. If we don't publish them I'm sure someone else will, and they might get good reviews, but to be honest I would never have finished reading them if I didn't have to." I pointed to the third manuscript. "This one is different. It's something new, and it's kind of exciting even though hardly anything happens. Like a crime novel without a crime."

In hindsight it seems to me that I wasn't exactly delivering original verdicts. Anyone with a little experience would presumably have said more or less the same, but in that moment I felt as if I'd been able to formulate my own opinion for the very first time.

Gunnar nodded.

"A crime novel without a crime," he said. "We'll use that on the back cover."

I laughed, relieved and confused, unsure if he was joking. But he wasn't.

"I'll take a look at it over the weekend, but I trust your judgment," he went on. "We have to publish a few debutants, and God knows hardly anybody can write these days. You can take care of this one if we decide to go with it."

"Okay," I said, still bewildered and with a whole series of objections lining up in my head—I can't, I'm too scared, my internship will be over long before this book goes to print—but I didn't dare say a word. Gunnar smiled his friendly but slightly impersonal smile, tossed the two rejected manuscripts into a cardboard box, and our meeting was over.

It's an embarrassing admission, but at the time I didn't really know who I was dealing with. He was an older man, and I was still young enough to think that most older men looked more or less the same. In my eyes there was nothing special about him. It wasn't until I began to do a little research into Gunnar Abrahamsson that I realized he was something of a celebrity within the industry. I felt stupid all over again, for not having grasped who he was, for being so unguarded when I spoke to him.

He had been one of the major stars in the publishing world in the eighties and nineties, when he discovered some of the authors who would go on to be among Sweden's greats. In the lunchroom there was a wall covered with old framed photographs and press cuttings that no one bothered to update anymore, and I noticed a picture of him from a Nobel banquet toward the end of the eighties. He had his arm around the shoulders of that year's winner of the Nobel Prize in Literature, and they were both beaming. Ten years earlier he had launched Andromeda, a book series featuring "the most interesting contemporary voices," as it says on the old covers, and in the majority of cases it was true. It was a beautiful imprint, designed with simplicity and unity, and it really did serve as a guide to authors who would be influential in the future. Many of today's great names began their literary career with Andromeda.

The imprint lived on, although its publications were sporadic now. Gunnar thought that much of what was written today didn't meet Andromeda's high standards, which were also his own high standards. Instead he devoted himself to looking after the authors he had cultivated from the start. His appearance was pretty ordinary, kind of anonymous because of his age and because of the boring, steel-rimmed glasses he wore, but he was tall and well-dressed, even though there was often something a little careless about his appearance: a handkerchief that looked as if it had been shoved into his breast pocket without much thought, a leather briefcase that had seen better days. Apparently he'd had heart problems, and according to the lunchtime gossip he was biding his time until retirement, when he and his wife were planning to move to their summer home in Provence.

Everything happened fast after our meeting. Gunnar beckoned me into his office one morning and told me that Jenny would be going on maternity leave, and that I was to take her place until she returned. Jenny was an editor, but she had started on her path toward a publishing post with a couple of books that had done well, and I knew that she was considered promising. I was also aware that things didn't usually happen like this, that there must be a procedure for the way vacant posts were advertised and filled. However, Gunnar was in a position to do as he wished, and it would be foolish for me to say no, even though the idea of saying yes was utterly terrifying. I convinced myself that I had nothing to lose; there wasn't much of my university course left, and I could always complete it later. What was the life of an impoverished student compared with a career at Rydéns? They published authors I had read and admired since I was a teenager, and now I might get the opportunity to work with them. Not to mention all the contacts I would be able to make, the situations I would be part of, and the parties, those legendary parties up on the roof. It was a dizzying invitation, a promise of a completely different life, exactly the kind of life I had wanted for so long. And so I said yes.

It is extraordinary how quickly we can adapt to the way we think others see us. When I first arrived at Rydéns I felt conscientious and anxious, I thought the others saw me as the hardworking student who had submitted the best application for the internship, irreproachable but incapable of contributing anything original. I believed my personality lacked a certain bohemian quality, an easygoing, comfortable approach that I envied in all those around me.

As soon as I was employed, I felt different. I started to think that the others must be wondering what qualities

I brought to the role. Why had I been given Jenny's job, when I hadn't even completed my internship and never said a word in meetings? Suddenly it seemed to me that next to them I came across as an amateur, insecure and unprofessional compared to the practiced ease with which they worked. That made me work much harder. I was often the last to leave in the evenings, and once I got home I almost always had a manuscript to read, to edit, to form an opinion of. I also read my way through the books published that season, both by Rydéns and other houses. I thought I needed to have an entire library in my head, I had to know who every author was and how they wrote, I needed to have read so much that I would instinctively know what was good and what was bad, what was on an upward trajectory and which trends were already over, that I had to understand the contemporary scene, understand the new writers, understand everything.

One day Gunnar asked me to sit in on a discussion with Amelie Stjärne, one of the authors he had discovered in the eighties. Back then she was young and radical, she wrote bold, revealing novels that were still read and loved by young women. Now she was almost sixty and had aged gently and with dignity, as wealthy people do, with beautifully cut hair and soft lines around her eyes.

"What a pretty blouse," Gunnar said when she had taken off her coat.

It really was a pretty blouse, some kind of Oriental pattern in muted colors, and he had the ability to deliver compliments as if he were making an obvious comment, something that no one could possibly take offense at.

Amelie smiled in delight.

"He always flatters me, that's why I've stayed with him," she said, winking at me.

I smiled back at her as if we were in cahoots, two women who both appreciated Gunnar's unassuming charm.

After making small talk about the coming summer and Amelie's house on the island of Gotland, Gunnar moved on to the half-finished manuscript she had submitted to him. It was like watching a dance, with Gunnar steering her so skillfully through what was actually quite harsh criticism that in the end it seemed as if she was the one who had come up with a plethora of fresh ideas during the conversation, she who had seen the fundamental changes she needed to make, she who had worked out how to revise and make cuts. He was present and attentive, and he had the ability to make her feel both seen and understood to such an extent that her cheeks were glowing. He gave her exactly the kind of attention that she and her manuscript required.

She left feeling overwhelmed and happy, knowing that she was a great author, that she had something within her that, with a little refinement, could become a great and significant novel.

Gunnar had created that novel, I thought. I pictured him sitting down with her flaky draft, asking himself what was the very best book that could be made of it, intuitively seeing the changes that were necessary to achieve that goal. And when I saw the sketches for the cover I thought that the author's name really ought to be Gunnar Abrahamsson, not Amelie Stjärne.

At the end of May I finally got to attend a party.

All day there was an atmosphere of carefree excitement in the office, a sense of anticipation which meant that no one could really concentrate on their work. The catering company staff were around all day, carrying tables up to the terrace, wheeling clothes racks into the cloakroom, and bringing in case after case of wine. As five o'clock approached the huge trays of food arrived, an early summer buffet provided by one of Stockholm's finest restaurants, salmon and crudités, small but beautifully decorated quiches, sauces and dips, tempting salads, freshly baked bread in great big baskets, and butter in little bowls. Then the teenage sons and daughters of Rydéns's employees showed up, ready to staff the cloakroom and help out during the evening. I changed into a new dress, new shoes, new earrings, and the guests began to arrive.

The whole thing was wonderful. It was exactly the way I wanted life to be, and I got to be the person I wanted to be: the hostess of a fantastic party, receiving the guests and chatting with them, making sure they had a glass of wine then ushering them into the festivities.

I felt proud and important. And I felt even more important later, when Gunnar had extricated himself from a long, drawn-out conversation and we stood together, talking to the authors we had worked with. Amelie Stjärne laughed at something he said, and Vilma Isaksson, who had written the first manuscript I'd recommended for publication, was noticeably nervous but gradually relaxed. The four of us were by the bar, and Gunnar said, "You see these coasters? They've been used ever since the very first parties at Rydéns. One was actually found among Strindberg's effects," and Vilma said, "But surely he wasn't published by Rydéns?" and Gunnar smiled and said, "No, but we've always thrown the best parties." And she laughed, both at the anecdote and because she was a part of something so desirable, and I laughed too for the same reasons, as the sun slowly dipped below the rooftops. The desserts were melting, the kids checking coats had managed to get tipsy, the world seemed to be enchanted, sparkling, wonderful.

Afterward I realized that all I had cared about that evening was Gunnar. Being close to him, standing beside him, observing how he spoke to the authors and made sure that they were enjoying themselves, that they felt part of something bigger.

I barely paid any attention to my colleagues. What did Andrea and Peter do all night? I exchanged a few words with Sally at the buffet, but that was mainly because I didn't have anyone else to talk to at the time, and in the lunchroom the following day, when everyone, slightly hungover, started cheerfully comparing notes on who they had spoken to—a literary critic from a major newspaper, the new girl in the children's department, a former

publisher from Rydéns who had moved into advertising—
I realized that I had no interest in what they were saying.
The only person I had wanted to talk to was Gunnar.

When autumn came that year it was wonderful, mild days
with the air shimmering like mother-of-pearl and twilights that slowly wrapped Stockholm in a warm darkness. I bought new clothes, because for the first time I had
a little money to play with, clothes that were appropriate
for working in an office, and I felt like an adult with my
monthly salary and my daily routines and the occasional
lunch in the city. I loved the corridors at Rydéns, the dark
wood and the bespoke tiles and mosaics, the beautiful ceiling lamps with their pleasant glow reflected in the brass.

The building was one of the highlights of Swedish
1960s architecture, so well-thought-out and executed
that we often had a group of trainee architects on a study
visit. Tourists would take photographs as they passed by.
I enjoyed carrying a pile of papers from the printer to my
desk, fetching a cup of coffee and drinking it by one of
the large windows overlooking the busy street. And most
of all I loved my job, the manuscripts I worked on. I loved
being involved in creating literature, and it seemed as if
the city sang to me while I walked home in the evenings,
sang with electricity and sirens, winked seductively with
traffic lights and neon signs. The feeling rubbed off on
the manuscripts I read, I felt intoxicated by an intense
lust for life and by insights I couldn't put into words, they
were utopian, they gave me a taste of how magnificent

and beautiful life could be, and I wanted literature to be like that too, as impactful as life itself when it was at its most powerful, and I wanted to be the one who made it that way.

"Do you have any plans for this afternoon? Or early evening?" Gunnar asked me one Thursday in October. As usual I didn't, apart from working, and just after three he appeared by my desk and said quietly that it was time for us to leave.

"Where are we going?" I asked.

"You'll see."

I picked up my coat and my purse and accompanied him out of the building, along Norrlandsgatan and through Kungsträdgården. It was a glorious autumn afternoon, the contours of the city had an unreal sharpness, the gulls flying over the water were brilliant white.

"This air is something else," Gunnar said, narrowing his eyes against the bright sunlight. "It's funny, this is how you imagine the autumn, and yet it's hardly ever exactly like this. I'd be surprised if it happens more than once a year."

When we reached the Royal Opera House, he strode over to the bistro known as Bakfickan and held the door open for me.

"Might not be the best place on a day like this," he said, nodding toward a small, dimly lit foyer, "but come on in."

The restaurant consisted of a single room that was almost empty. The lunchtime diners had left, and those who wanted a drink after work wouldn't be here for at least an hour. The sun couldn't find its way in through the windows and the light inside was warm and subdued, creating a relaxed atmosphere. A waiter was polishing glasses and chatting with a chef. They both smiled when we walked in.

"How's it going?" the waiter asked.

"Can't complain," Gunnar replied.

"What can I get you today?"

"I believe you have a new Chablis?"

Gunnar took off his coat and hung it on a hook on the wall, then sat down at the table farthest in. I took the seat opposite him as the waiter appeared with a bottle and two glasses. After the little ritual when Gunnar tasted the wine and said, "Excellent," and the waiter poured us each a glass then left the bottle in a ice bucket on the table, silence fell. I found the situation quite stressful. Were the two of us going to drink an entire bottle of wine? That would take ages. How was I going to converse with him for such a long time without him realizing that I was boring, without my saying something dumb? Or maybe someone else was joining us? That would make things easier, yet there was something strangely flattering about the idea that it was just Gunnar and me, that for some reason he had chosen my company.

He raised his glass to me in a toast before we tried the wine.

"Not bad at all," he said.

"It's delicious," I replied.

That was an understatement, it was the best wine I'd ever drunk.

He smiled and immediately looked more relaxed than he usually did in the office, when he often came across as very serious and a little cantankerous.

We had sent a book to the printer the previous day, and he told me a story about when he first started at Rydéns and almost missed a spelling error in the title on a front cover, then he moved on to another anecdote about the book's author and his habit of taking his dog along to every meeting and personal appearance. I don't know where the time went. Afterward I thought about the meeting with Amelie Stjärne, the way Gunnar led her through the conversation as if it were a dance. He did the same with me over the wine, occasionally asking discreet questions that made me talk about myself honestly and candidly. Several times he laughed at something I said. It felt as if the universe contracted around us and we were its innermost core, a bubble of unexpected intimacy and slight intoxication that was a lovely place to be.

Suddenly the bottle was empty and twilight was beginning to fall outside.

I was almost embarrassed at having talked so much, at having felt close to him so quickly, and our leave-taking was a little awkward. He was obviously in a hurry but didn't want to rush our goodbyes. When we parted he set off briskly along Fredsgatan.

It wasn't until I was walking through the Old Town that I realized I hadn't thanked him for the wine. I sent a text, possibly a bit warmer than if I hadn't been tipsy: "Forgot to say thank you for the wine. Thank you! I really enjoyed myself."

His reply came in less than a minute: "I enjoyed myself too."

I looked at the brief message, looked at it over and over again during the course of the evening as I wandered around at home with another glass of wine in my hand because it was still early and I was restless, excited. He had enjoyed himself too.

It was clear right from the start that Gunnar and I worked well together. We could be open with each other in a way that meant there was no friction between us. The differences of opinion that did arise were usually fruitful, and never turned into a symbolic power struggle. He often gave me a task that I would silently protest, thinking I couldn't do it, but then I would execute it nervously and conscientiously, because I couldn't bear to disappoint him, and he would say, "Well done," and I would drink in his praise. I understood that he was testing me, and that he was doing so because for some reason he had decided to believe in me.

During the autumn he allowed me to edit the next book in the Andromeda imprint, and we spent many hours going over the manuscript together. I was convinced that it could be improved if we got rid of the irritating hesitation that I felt pervaded the text. He understood what I meant, and the two of us came up with a number of suggested changes. I was tasked with going through these suggestions with Jesper Ask, the author, whose debut novel had attracted widespread acclaim a few years earlier.

When Jesper and I were sitting opposite each other at a big table in one of the conference rooms I thought about how Gunnar handled his authors, how he managed to make every criticism constructive, how he always made the writers think that the ideas he presented were their own, how he filled them with trust and self-confidence. And eventually I had gotten Jesper exactly where I wanted him: He thought my proposed changes made a lot of sense, he completely agreed about the hesitation in the manuscript, and he assured me that he would go straight home and revise the text. He left the meeting straight-backed and with resolve in his step. From the window of the conference room I watched him make his way among the pedestrians down below, filled with the sense that he was about to produce something great.

It was a few weeks before I received an amended version of his manuscript. At first I thought he had accidentally attached the wrong document. There was hardly any difference from the original version, and almost none of the issues I found problematic had been addressed. "I'm not sure if I've received the right version," I wrote to him, "could you resend the new one?" But as I'd suspected, there was no mistake.

"I don't know what he's been doing," I said wearily to Gunnar.

"It happens sometimes," he said. "I'm sure Jesper believes he's made major changes. I don't think he has the capacity to see what it is that needs changing, even though you've explained it to him. There's a difference between understanding in theory, and actually being able to achieve something when you're sitting there with the text in front of you."

"So what do I do now?" I could hear how tired I sounded, like a whining toddler, but I really was disappointed. I'd been looking forward to working on Andromeda, and now my first book was going to be a fiasco.

Gunnar shrugged. "It's too late to reject the manuscript now, so you'll have to give it another go if you think it will help. I'm afraid there's no alternative."

He went off to one of his frequent lunches. If he wasn't meeting an author, then it was someone else in the publishing industry or a former colleague, he had a huge network of contacts that I reckoned were just that—contacts, not friends. Regular lunches to keep up with developments in the world of publishing and the cultural climate in general.

I went to the lunchroom, got my sandwich from the refrigerator and took it back to my desk, opened up Jesper's manuscript again. He had called it *Quiet Wind*, a somewhat pretentious title for a somewhat pretentious narrative about a father and son, but it suited the tone of the novel, since everything was solemn but fleeting. I slowly scrolled through the pages. It was like a film that needed to be rearranged and shortened, not to mention the many sentences that needed to be changed in order to give the impression that a writer with real authority was telling the story. There is no difference between fiction and reality in that respect: If you appear to be confident enough in what you're saying, then people will believe you.

I placed the cursor in the text and dragged it over a section, which I deleted with one decisive click. I scrolled down, highlighted another section, deleted that too. It felt like clearing an overgrown patch in the garden; as soon as the superfluous text was gone, what remained stood out as both clearer and better. I deleted one more paragraph, moved another. When I had a structure I was happy with, I changed the tense throughout the manuscript from past to present. It took a while, but it brought a freshness, a new energy. Then I began to alter all the phrases that annoyed me. I realized I had forgotten about my sandwich. I picked it up and distractedly took a few bites before forgetting about it again. Working on Jesper's text was like entering a state I remembered from my childhood—being completely absorbed in the imaginary world I had created, not noticing the passage of time. Like a dream with total presence, a perfect intoxication.

"I'm leaving now." Gunnar had suddenly appeared beside me. He was wearing his coat and carrying his old briefcase.

"Okay."

Dusk had fallen, the lights of the city were sparkling out there. I felt as if I'd just woken up, my cheeks were burning.

"What time is it?" I asked.

"Five thirty. What are you doing?"

"It's... I'm just doing some edits on Jesper's manuscript," I mumbled.

"See you tomorrow," Gunnar said, heading for the elevator.

As the time approached nine o'clock and I finally began to feel as if the end were in sight, it seemed to me that this was the most satisfying thing I had done in my adult life. I had created clarity, structure, credibility. I had written a novel.

"I took the liberty of making a few changes," I wrote to Jesper. "They're only suggestions—take a look and see what you think."

The reply arrived at midnight, when I had gone to bed but was still too excited to sleep.

"Brilliant," he wrote. "Now it's finished!"

I thought *Quiet Wind* was the most perfect book I had ever seen. The design of the Andromeda imprint followed a strict template, but all the books had a picture on the cover that distinguished them from one another. We had chosen a slightly blurred photograph that looked a bit like an unsuccessful snap from a family album: a little boy sitting on a man's knee, both of them looking straight at the camera, yet somehow cut off from the world by the lack of focus. Andromeda's small logo gleamed on the back, a stylized star constellation in gold.

"I didn't actually take the name Andromeda from the constellation," Gunnar said. "It's from a line by Sappho."

"Oh?"

"*Andromeda has something better to offer.* Andromeda is another woman, I think it was written out of jealousy. Occasionally I've thought that maybe it's a bit irreverent to use it to sell books, but then no one knows that's where the name comes from. And I also wanted to have something better to offer."

"You could regard it as a tribute," I suggested.

"I do. You know, it's hard to find something that deals with life in such a genuine way as Sappho's poetry, and yet it consists almost entirely of fragments. You get the high and then the low, the superficial and words that really mean something. The complexity of a human being. Sometimes I've thought..." He paused for a moment. "Sometimes I've thought that those disjointed segments are so powerful because that's the way life is. That's how you remember it with hindsight, like a series of fragments. Reading Sappho is like reliving your life, in a concentrated form. Being confronted by what you recall, for better or worse."

"Maybe it's just as well that there are only fragments," I said. "Imagine if there had been a whole lot of complete poems, and she was nowhere near as good as she appears to be? Everything seems interesting when you don't know much about it. And everyone. It's so easy to romanticize another person from a distance, only to be disappointed when you actually get to know her. Because the parts were more interesting than the whole."

The words came spilling out, I hadn't given them any thought, but he gazed at me for a long time. I recognized that look, it was the one he got when he was beginning to doubt his own conviction. It didn't happen very often, but I knew I wanted to be the person who evoked that look.

One morning Gunnar met me at my desk and informed me that *Quiet Wind* had been nominated for a major literary prize. At first I found it difficult to process the idea that something I was a part of could reach such a level. The highest level. Then I noticed the way my colleagues were looking at me, and decided to enjoy the nomination and the attention, just like they would have. They weren't exactly churlish, and they all congratulated me, but I could tell that there was something about the whole thing that bothered them—presumably me.

Gunnar was clearly happy to see my happiness, but he took it all calmly, almost with a kind of ironic distance, even though the nomination had added another gold star to his tally as well.

"Don't forget, a nomination isn't an objective endorsement of a book's quality," he said. "Those juries are always as corrupt as hell."

"To our advantage, in that case," I replied.

He smiled. "Well done," he murmured, as if it went against the grain to offer praise, although it was clear from his tone that he meant it.

I knew he didn't regard *Quiet Wind* as a particularly good novel, but he was making a real effort not to say something even more acerbic, for my sake, and I think he could see that I understood.

I slowly began to realize that he wasn't uncontroversial, even within Rydéns. The publishing choices he made were largely based on his own taste and intuition, and he made no secret of the fact that he had a low opinion of any other parameters. For example, he despised anything to do with celebrities, frequently complaining about interviews with actors and pop stars in magazines and on TV. At one of our editorial meetings Andrea revealed that a young woman with a very popular blog had submitted a really good novel, and Gunnar rolled his eyes discreetly. Then again, he saw no intrinsic value in material that appealed only to a niche market; he could equally have rolled his eyes at conceptual poetry. He felt that literature should not distance itself from its readers, yet he recoiled from anything with a whiff of mainstream or bestseller. His own taste lay somewhere in the middle, literature that appealed to an educated reading public that barely existed anymore.

It seemed to me that the sun-bleached postcard stuck on the wall above his desk, an academic nineteenth-century painting of Pygmalion kissing life into his ivory-white statue, wasn't there by chance. Maybe that was how he saw himself: almost as much of an author as the authors themselves, sometimes even more. And in my eyes that was absolutely true. It was Gunnar who kissed life into their half-finished manuscripts, took them from adequate to magnificent, Gunnar who turned them into literature.

During that autumn we established a tradition, leaving work shortly after three o'clock every other Thursday.

"We have a meeting," Gunnar would announce in the beginning, just in case anyone wondered where we were, but soon it became a routine that everyone knew about, and no announcement was necessary.

I enjoyed our strolls to Bakfickan. As the weeks passed, the sprawling, bare branches of the trees stood out against the darkening sky, the streetlamps in Kungsträdgården came on earlier and earlier, their glow reflected in the rain-soaked cobbles. It almost felt as if we were in a different, bigger city, in Paris or Berlin, and that feeling lingered in the restaurant, where we always sat at the same table and Gunnar ordered a bottle of wine.

He worked from home every other Friday, and after our meetings he continued to the central station and got on the train to Gnesta, where he and his wife, Marianne, had a house. They usually spent weekends there, and Marianne was sometimes there during the week as well. She was the editor of an interior-design magazine and could often work remotely.

Gunnar had no children of his own, but Marianne had three sons. For reasons that weren't entirely clear he didn't have a very high opinion of them, he would alternate between referring to them in a slightly jokey tone as bone idle and careerists—the worst insults he could come up with. He might well have been right in both respects. From the little he told me, they came across as spoiled and superficial, but on the other hand I knew that Gunnar was critical of everyone, and that his verdict didn't necessarily mean a great deal. Laziness, however, was a particular bugbear of his. He had always worked hard and valued those who did the same without making a big deal of it. He wasn't interested in hearing others brag about their achievements, and was always quick to label anyone he thought lacked substance and a willingness to work as a "big mouth" and a "poser." There was an old-fashioned, hardworking aspect to his character, possibly a legacy from the agricultural Sweden of days gone by that was a part of his background.

He had grown up in Älvsjö as the only child of a single mother, who'd had him when she was very young. She had moved from her parents' farm in Södermanland to look for work in the city, and more or less by chance she had ended up with the Customs Service, where she had stayed for the rest of her life. Gunnar had worked during every school vacation since his early teens. One summer in the seventies he had applied for a job at Rydéns and had been hired as a mail boy in the big, newly founded publishing house. He read enough of their output to form an opinion on it, and one of the bosses had taken him seriously when they happened to fall into conversation. Soon Gunnar was transferred to the fiction department. That kind of thing could easily happen back then, and I knew that he still wanted that kind of thing to happen, which was why I had been offered the post at Rydéns.

Eventually he became the editor in chief, and for a number of years his voice was heard in cultural debates. "Classic Storytelling Is a Cornerstone of Democracy"— that was the somewhat overblown headline of an article he had written toward the end of the eighties, which I found in the archive of one of the broadsheets. He argued in favor of exactly the type of literature he was paid to publish, a fact that was wearily pointed out in the response from his opponent, a radical young poet. In an article about the publishing world a few years later, Gunnar was referred to as "the demon publisher." It was hard to see anything demonic about his mild-mannered personality, but on the other hand it was impossible to deny that he was behind several of Sweden's most successful authors in the eighties and nineties, a string of future winners of the August Prize, members of the Swedish Academy, professors, and important intellectuals.

I often wondered about his private life, he was very discreet about it. I had seen Marianne once when she met him at work, she looked exactly as I expected: blond, well-groomed, dressed almost entirely in black, but with a slightly sporty air, as if there were something healthy and robust about her that couldn't be suppressed by the color black. I had already realized that Gunnar appreciated women who made an effort with their appearance, but I still found it difficult to believe that she was his type. A man like Gunnar ought to want someone more mysterious, someone with an aura of Continental elegance rather than bourgeois rebellion and a membership in the Lidingö Golf Club.

Then again, maybe it was logical. He was comfortable among the upper classes; he never hid the fact that he liked money. He devoted his everyday life to work, but after that he wanted good food and good wine, the good life. He was interested in cooking, and enjoyed spending the weekends in Gnesta over a slow-cooked stew, a lamb shank, an ox cheek, while sipping a glass of wine from his extensive collection. I was aware that he had traveled a great deal, he often mentioned cities in other countries as if he knew them as well as Stockholm, but he never gave the impression of showing off. He liked to talk about things that meant a lot to him: Renaissance art, Proust, fishing, Benny Goodman, a bistro he always went to in Paris.

I imagined that he and Marianne had a nice, if somewhat shallow existence together. She was outgoing, sorted out their social life in the way that wives do. Occasionally he would complain because she had arranged a dinner with people he referred to as idiots, but at the same time he seemed to appreciate the effort she had made. I often wondered what they talked about, both with their friends and when the two of them were alone. From what I had gathered, she wasn't particularly interested in literature, except for the odd crime novel when she was on vacation, or a biography to provide a topic of conversation during those dinners. Her field was interior design, and she seemed to have spent a great deal of both time and money getting their three homes the way she wanted them. Gunnar went along with it as long as she didn't interfere with his bookshelves and allowed him to hang a painting or two that he liked.

They spent the summers at their house in Provence, plus the odd week during the autumn and spring. The plan was to live there as much as possible in the future. Marianne was the driving force, but once again Gunnar didn't object. He was adaptable without being a doormat, somehow kind of homeless in life, and I sometimes thought maybe that was why he had spent the whole of his career in the same place: because the books he worked with at Rydéns were the closest thing he had to a home.

One afternoon he told me about the great reading experiences of his youth, about the summer when he worked as a night porter and read Dostoyevsky, the summer he worked as a sexton and read Thomas Mann, the summer he worked as a subway station attendant and read Proust. It was the latter that moved him the most, he talked at length about time and nostalgia, about trying to catch ahold of something that was lost forever.

"It's tragic, really," he said, "how lonely we are with so many of our memories. All those things that meant such a lot to us, the little details that combine to make up almost everything that is precious in life. A scent, an atmosphere, a particular kind of light in the sky. All those fleeting elements that can't be re-created. Books hold so many memories, details that live on because someone has tried to put them into words, written them down and woven them into a narrative. Just imagine how many perceptions of the world are passed on from one person to another."

There was a special tone in his voice when he approached certain topics. He still spoke quietly, but with real passion, a softly glowing conviction. I think I felt closest to him when he talked about literature, because everything he said I had also experienced but had been unable to express. How life-changing a reading experience can be, how it can fill you with a completely new perception of what life could be, fresh insights into what is worth striving for, worth believing in and defending, what it means to live life to the fullest. I realized that for both of us, something had been missing before those key reading experiences, and that the same would always be true from then on. It was like having fought in a war and being injured, carrying lifelong damage. And yet his driving force was a kind of restlessness, a constant search for the next writer who might come close to what had really meant something to him, a longing to be injured again.

He talked about literature with a certain solemnity, but he didn't put it on a pedestal. It was more that he saw it as a powerful force, but also the highest expression of civilization, a mixture of an almost biologically determined mechanism and one of the most refined ways of rising above nature that humanity had achieved. He often returned to myths and legends, the themes that had their origins in the dawn of history, questions that he regarded as an inescapable element of what it means to be a human being.

"Good literature almost always has a trace of that," he said. "Including contemporary writing. It usually makes its presence felt through a sense of inevitability. It's hard to explain more clearly, but if you have the ability to pick up on it, then you will notice it when you're reading. You are aware of an archaic trace within the story, the residue of something ancient that lingers in our own time."

"Like the tailbone," I said.

He looked at me, surprised but amused. "The tailbone?"

"Yes—you know, rudiments that remain in the body from earlier stages of development. We no longer have a tail, but the tailbone is still there."

He smiled. "All good literature has a tailbone," he said.

On another afternoon he told me that he used to work in the stock room at the NK department store in the late sixties and developed a taste for elegant clothing, which was at odds with the zeitgeist back then.

"I spent almost the whole of my last paycheck on a suit," he said, with a boyish, delighted smile. "I got a staff discount, plus a little extra off the price because the manager of the menswear department had seen me lusting after it every day during my lunch break, and felt sorry for me."

And so he stepped out into the revolutionary cultural landscape dressed in a beige suit with a discreet houndstooth pattern.

It was typical of him, typical of the subtle contrariness that pervaded his character, he wanted to own exclusive clothes even though he regarded such things as hopelessly bourgeois. He could speak with real feeling about the power of literature at one moment, and the next he was talking about the desire for a smart suit.

I wondered what he had been like as a young man, how others had viewed him. It was hard to imagine him in such a politicized era, and I still couldn't quite place him politically. Maybe he was a conservative Social Democrat, or a social democratically inclined Conservative; he disliked cheery liberalism, yet he believed in the individual.

He often talked about himself but never got too personal. He skillfully avoided any obvious pressure points. I sensed that this was because he simply couldn't bring himself to go near them, that he was still too heavily influenced by his heritage, by a working-class older generation and their inability to talk about feelings. Instead he made it seem like a point of honor not to talk about such things. The dignified way of handling something as irrational as emotions was not to ask questions, not to explain, to leave everything unspoken. Maybe that was also an expression of his view on a gentleman's discretion: It was civilized for certain things to remain implicit.

Sometimes I thought that there must be things he might have benefited from articulating, the things I wondered about but never dared to ask: Had he ever met his father? Had he wanted children of his own, and how come it had never happened? Was he happy in his marriage? Certain topics were inaccessible, as if they were locked in a cabinet with such a complicated system of compartments and drawers that it wasn't even worth trying.

He never said anything negative about feminism, but he never said anything positive either. It was a question that simply didn't seem to concern him, just like party politics. It was hard to imagine him voting at all, it seemed way too vulgar. Dignity was paramount. He was a melancholy person, perhaps even a pessimist, and a romantic, as the biggest pessimists often are. He had high ideals, which meant that he was constantly disappointed, whether it concerned society, people, art, or literature, but he also never stopped hoping that something better was possible. There was a brusqueness about him, an unpolished element that made him both human and slightly scary, until you realized that the sudden outbursts and curses were mostly jargon. In fact he rarely got angry for real and was usually in a good mood.

"Don't think you'll learn anything about literature there," he would say when I mentioned the university. "You learn by reading and living." Or: "You should respect education, but don't allow yourself to be intimidated by it. If only you knew how badly many academics write."

He would give his subdued but heartfelt laugh.

I felt proud to be sitting there with him. I felt like the person I wanted to be. Someone who goes to the Opera Bar with an educated older man and drinks wine a little too early in the afternoon. It was like a scene from a movie or a novel, a fictional insert in real life, just the way I had always wanted: urbane and cultured, an exception to the everyday, a sense that the unexpected could occur at any

moment. I was almost always the only woman in Bakfickan, the other customers tended to be pairs of suit-clad
men who snuck in for a plate of beef Rydberg or an early
beer after work. The restaurant was quiet, the decor well-
thought-out and beautiful, I understood that it was a place
you kept coming back to once you had learned to appreciate it.

Perhaps Gunnar also felt proud to be sitting there with
someone like me, who wanted to listen to him. Afterward
I would think that those hours were an extension of the
work we did at Rydéns, but instead of creating literature
we were creating each other. For a while both he and I
could be the people we wanted to be.

We joked about our meetings now and again, as if
we knew that the energy that sparked between us had
something unreliable about it, almost as if it had a will
of its own.

"Okay, I've finished indoctrinating you for today," he
might say with a little smile when it was almost time to say
goodbye, as if to take the sting out of the situation, frame it
in casual terms that neither of us really believed in.

"I love it when men explain things to me," I replied,
and we both laughed because it sounded like a joke, even
though it wasn't.

Our entire relationship was a silent protest against
everything we both loathed about the contemporary era:
the vulgar feminism, the tabloid rhetoric, the politiciza-
tion of every aspect of our lives, the commercialization of
the true and the beautiful, the narrow-minded assumption

that an older man and a younger woman couldn't possibly enjoy a mutual exchange because the balance of power was so obviously not in my favor. He was a man more than twice my age, he was my boss, and he was the one who paid for the wine. These circumstances almost guaranteed that I was being exploited or was trying to exploit him, as if the kind of relationship we had couldn't possibly exist without ulterior motives, without a measure of dishonesty.

There was nothing dishonest between us, quite the reverse: We were both searching for something genuine, and we found it in each other. Never has the phrase "balance of power" seemed less appropriate to describe what went on during those afternoons. That concept belonged to the engineers of emotion who have gained far too much influence these days, we were agreed on that, words included in a blurb on the back cover of a novel written for people like that, a novel that confirms their perception of the balance of power in certain types of relationships, not to mention that the world at large, on a structural level, is destructive and ought to be changed, renegotiated.

That was the kind of thing we talked about. We agreed that we would never allow a blurb with the words "balance of power" to get through. Was there a more boring phrase, a term that more accurately captured everything that was rigid and humorless about our times? Literature has to be bigger than that.

Gunnar and I understood that. The number crunchers—which was what he called everyone who talked about finances at Rydéns—definitely didn't. It was an unusual attitude, to be an editor at a publishing house without being driven by the desire to sell books, to despise those who did want to sell, but it always seemed to me that he probably identified more with the authors.

"You don't offer congratulations on good reviews," he once said. "It's patronizing to everyone who has worked on a novel, especially the author. A good book has its own value, irrespective of what someone who happens to write in a newspaper happens to think of it. If they even write what they really think. Usually they write what they're expected to think. It's hypocritical to congratulate someone on good reviews, you are joining in a game where the opinions of others, their approval, is ascribed a significance that they absolutely do not have."

"But what if it really is a good review?" I said. "If it's written by a critic you respect, and he or she has actually understood the book? If the author feels understood, as if they have sent their novel out into the world like a message in a bottle, and someone out there has found it?"

Gunnar shrugged. "That's never the reason why anyone says congratulations," he said, but I thought he sounded slightly less dogmatic. "You say it because someone whose opinions are totally uninteresting has publicly endorsed the book."

A recurring topic was the fact that so many of those who worked with literature didn't really care about it but simply regarded it as a job, a possible career path, which in turn led to a fundamentally dishonest relationship with it. "He doesn't understand what literature is," was a verdict he often delivered, or "She's not an intellectual person."

If the publishing world had ever been populated by intellectuals who understood what literature was, then that was definitely no longer the case. He never said it outright, but he was obviously both sad and angry that the world in which he had spent his entire professional life had changed so quickly, that the power had shifted from literature to money. He was the editor in chief, but his sphere of influence had gradually been curtailed. He wanted to continue working in the same way as when he entered the industry, making instant decisions, having the scope to take risks, a straightforward chain from signing a contract to publication. Nowadays everything had to pass through the finance and marketing departments, both staffed by people of whom he had a very low opinion.

Those afternoons at Bakfickan were like a strange pocket in time, Gunnar's role at Rydéns and the way he worked. I realized that its days were numbered, that it was a leftover fragment of an era that was already lost, a beautiful little enclave of what used to be a magnificent empire but was now a dwindling catalog, key account managers, and blog breakfasts. It seemed to me that Gunnar must be aware of that too, deep down.

He once told me about Florence during the Second World War. In order to save the city's art treasures from Allied bombing, all the smaller pieces had been transported out into the Tuscan countryside and hidden in houses and barns. Some of Michelangelo's sculptures from the Galleria dell'Accademia, *David* for example, were too heavy to move, and instead they built brick walls around them. They looked like great big beehives or strange pre-historic buildings, and there they stood, the pinnacle of the Italian Renaissance, protected from attack.

He found it touching that people had made such an effort to save the best of what their predecessors had created. I couldn't help thinking that he felt an affinity with something in this story, that he saw a parallel between what he had built up and Michelangelo's sculptures. A part of him wished that his life's work could also be protected from the depredations of the modern day.

He might have realized that his time was running out, but he was determined that certain things would endure: the way he ran Andromeda, his belief in literature, his contempt for commercialism and superficiality. His values fulfilled a higher purpose that must continue to be fulfilled, even when he was no longer there.

"You do realize," he said one afternoon in the bar, "that you're the one who will have to take over when I'm gone."

It was a statement rather than a question, a fact I had never considered. Partly because it was hard to imagine a day when Gunnar and I were no longer united against the world, and partly because I was so wet behind the ears. In comparison with the knowledge and experience he had acquired, I was nothing.

"Seriously?" I said.

It was a somewhat coquettish response, but explicit affirmation from him was so rare that I wanted to suck it up when it was on offer.

"I'll make sure of it," he said.

"One of the biggest mistakes of our time," he said one afternoon as we were getting to the bottom of the bottle of wine, "is that nostalgia has been turned into a taboo."

I had never thought of him as a particularly nostalgic person, quite the reverse in fact, nor did I have much time for nostalgia. My whole life had been about a constant forward motion, a belief—swinging between vague hope and strong conviction—that things would get better, or if not better, then at least they would be different, and this difference had an intrinsic value, because the idea that everything would carry on as it had originally been was too depressing.

"I don't mean we should wallow in the past," he said. "In fact I'm not talking about nostalgia on a personal level at all. It's about a sense of humility when it comes to history, a humility that should be taken seriously. For a long time nostalgia has been depicted as something destructive, politically dangerous even. In a way that's true, of course: nostalgia cannot be allowed to direct the course of society. However, to suppress that feeling is to give away all its inherent strength to powers that neither deserve nor can handle it, but will exploit it for their own ends. You know, it's easy to make fun of those who think we can learn something from history. They always come across as kind of foolish, compared to all those who are in favor of the new. But for people like you and me"—he caught my gaze and held it until the increasingly charged atmosphere made me look away—"there is a home in history. For those of us who come from generations lost to oblivion, generations that have never distinguished themselves, never lived lives that were worth documenting, left no real traces behind. For us, history is important, it provides a context. It is important to respect the need for context. It is an incredibly powerful need."

He reached for the bottle in the silver bucket and poured the last of the wine into our glasses. Outside the afternoon's drizzle had turned into a downpour, hammering against the windows. We were the only guests in the restaurant and it felt like our castle, our fortress against the world.

"Do you know something else that benefits from a dislike of nostalgia?" he went on. "Capitalism. It is a nonproductive emotion, it doesn't generate profit for anyone. Even so, it is the left that has the biggest problem with nostalgia. I find it very strange, the left and neoliberals uniting in their fear of nostalgia, of tradition, the old. They want new people, new markets."

He might not have regarded himself as particularly left wing, but he often spoke contemptuously about capitalism, although what he actually meant was probably commercialism. It didn't matter, we both knew what he meant and we were in agreement.

I also realized that what he called nostalgia was re-
lated to a sense that something had been lost, both in
time and in history, perhaps ultimately in himself. This
"something" was abstract and difficult to articulate, it
was easy to undermine such a vague feeling with rational
arguments about social progress. I found it moving that
he was prepared to talk to me about an issue that clearly
touched him on such a personal level. I hoped he had
chosen to do so because he thought I would understand
him, which I did.

Both of us came from nothing, and in a way we were
nobodies: We operated in the shadows, we had no desire to
assert ourselves, no need to position ourselves at the center. My background was nothing special, just a perfectly
normal Swedish upbringing. An ordinary house in an area
where houses were cheap, playgrounds with swings made
out of tires, the mixed forests of central Sweden, a 1970s
grade school dropped like a barracks in the middle of a
field, parents who dutifully went off to work without any
particular career ambitions, the school library and public swimming pools, grated carrot salad and breaded fish,
spring twilights at the fast-food stall, boys on mopeds.
A small, neat, tidy existence, pleasant and safe, but like
a capricious god it demanded sacrifices, swallowing up
those who remained, dragging down those who didn't
keep moving.

I had spent my whole life running as if I were racing
across day-old ice, fleeing from the wolves panting down
the back of my neck, their breath redolent of small towns,

the working class. As time went by I noticed that many people in Stockholm had the same drive, everyone had their own wolves. They all wanted to feel that they had reached their goals through their own efforts, that they had finally achieved what they thought they deserved.

"Bear" and "burden" have the same root, it is such a beautiful literal twist: you bear your inheritance, you carry the burden, the random creation of the generations that went before you. A yoke to some, a ticket to the world for others. Gunnar and I bear the same burden: We constantly feel like strangers in the world we have entered, the world we saw shimmering on the horizon and ran toward. I could understand his nostalgia from that perspective, the sense that something had been lost, that we had exchanged a home for a life of homelessness. We had attained the greatest freedom, but at the same time we were faced with its downside—loneliness. We were two people who would always be fundamentally lonely, and we recognized that aspect of each other: The same fate that had once pushed us toward literature had pushed us toward each other.

"There's something Faustian about it," he once said when we were sitting in the armchairs in his office, "about the deal we struck when we swapped what we came from for this."

He spread his arms wide, taking in the overstuffed bookshelves, and gave me a gentle, melancholy smile.

Together we became a unit, the two of us against the world. We would laugh at something the other person said, just like in the infatuation phase of a new relationship, when you laugh and think, "Wow—you're so funny and yet you want to be with me, I'm the one who gets to spend time with you." When something good happened we immediately wanted to tell each other, because we knew that the joy on hearing the news would be genuine and untrammeled, without that tiny hint of envy or resentment that can exist even in firm friendships and romantic relationships. I knew that Gunnar respected me. He would never have said it out loud, because he just didn't say that kind of thing, but I was certain that the respect I felt for him was mutual.

"Go carefully," I said one evening as we parted company, the February slush had frozen to form a thick covering of ice on the sidewalks. I said it out of genuine concern, but in return I received one of his slightly noncommittal smiles, which often confused me. In hindsight it seems to me that he didn't want such exhortations. They reminded him of his age, of the fact that he was old enough for a fall on an icy sidewalk to be serious bad news, and he didn't want me to point that out. Maybe above all he didn't want to be reminded of the significant age gap between us.

"Have a nice weekend," we always said on Thursday evenings, and I wondered whether, like me, he thought it was just an empty phrase. Because even if we simply wanted each other's weekends to be nice, I always thought it would have been nicer if he didn't have to rush off to catch the train to Gnesta, climb aboard, and disappear to

a different life. Nicer if he could somehow have spent the
weekend with me.

We were usually in touch again before long. Sometimes he
would send a text message from the train, if he thought of
something he wanted to add to whatever we had been discussing. Otherwise he would contact me if he came across
a review of one of Rydéns's books, or if a columnist referred to them. He was often annoyed by the bad reviews,
but almost as often by the good ones. He would say that
the reviewer clearly hadn't understood the book, or that the
reading was tendentious or ideological. Perhaps he felt that
the book was praised for the wrong reasons, sometimes dia-
metrically opposed to our reasons for publishing it.

"Pearls before swine," he would comment. Or: "At
least the number crunchers will be happy."

My role was to agree and fan the flames of his anger,
which bound us together even more tightly, or to try to
calm him. A wife's job, I thought occasionally, wondering
what life was like out there in Gnesta, what Marianne was
doing while Gunnar was reading the paper.

One of his quirks was that he liked to discuss the weather.
It wasn't a topic for small talk as far as he was concerned,
nor was his principal interest in unusual events, in record
temperatures or wind speed or rainfall. The weather was
important to him.

"You know," he said, "it always irritates me when
someone insists on pointing out that talking about the

weather is boring, claims that it's typically Swedish because we're a land of farmers. I'm sure it's true to a certain extent, in countries where the weather is more stable and there isn't such a big difference between the seasons and urban life has existed for longer, I suppose there's no reason to talk about it. But here, most of us were farmers only a few generations back. My maternal grandparents were born in the nineteenth century, they had hardly any books in the house apart from the Bible, and they did nothing but work. The weather ruled their lives—what each day was going to be like, how the harvest would turn out, what the future would be. A rainy summer wasn't problematic because the vacation didn't meet expectations, it was a disaster because it put their whole existence at risk. They didn't have vacations."

He always spoke calmly, never tried to convince me of anything.

"When Mom and I went to visit them, we often spoke about the weather. No one perceived it as small talk, as if we should really have been discussing something else. In the summer we would sit in the arbor where it was generally cool, but one year there was a heat wave. Grandma had set out a plate of buns and cookies, and the frosting melted. She always put one of those mesh covers over the food and the flies were crawling across it—the heat had taken its toll on them too. We talked about the drought."

He fell silent.

"You have to respect your history," he said after a moment. "Especially people like us."

The part of the story that made the strongest impression on me was that he thought there was an us.

"You know," he said on another occasion, almost in passing, "life isn't as long as it seems. Make the most of it."

It was actually a relevant piece of advice for me, but I couldn't really take it in. There were times when I thought it was strange how little I needed. I was like one of those plants you can keep in an office for ages, standing in LECA beneath a sunlamp and producing greenery year after year. My life was ascetic and predictable, time oddly suspended as I watched people around me moving forward, toward new training and new jobs, new families, new phases in their lives.

I met up with my old friends from the university now and again, I would listen to them talking about taking new jobs, renovating their apartments, getting engaged, and becoming pregnant. I was always happy for them, yet I felt as if none of it really had anything to do with me. As if the kind of lives most people led were irrelevant to me. They were pleased for me too, happy that I had a good job I enjoyed, but I suspect they wondered if something wasn't missing: a drive, a momentum.

Personally, I didn't give it much thought. I had found a fixed point in my life, maybe for the first time ever. Sometimes it seemed strange that I was so absorbed in my work, that I felt so keenly alive under circumstances that on paper looked like nothing special. In many ways it was a shadowy existence.

But that was exactly how I felt. I went home in the evenings thinking I could hear the music of the spheres, an echo from space that touched something deep within me, a kind of harmony with the universe, there was nothing more to long for.

The summers were different, I missed him then. He and Marianne spent their entire vacation in Provence, and his text messages were sporadic. Presumably there were limited opportunities to sit in peace with his phone, maybe his days were filled with activities: visits to the beach when he left the phone at home, dinner in restaurants, socializing with the many friends I knew they had in France.

One day when Gunnar was eating in the lunchroom, unusually for him, someone had asked about his plans for the summer. He had talked about the house and its surroundings in rather muted terms, as if he wanted to spare me the most delightful details. I said I'd love to see a field of lavender some day.

At the end of July I received a postcard. It was beautiful in a kitsch way, a lilac-blue field of lavender in full bloom. "*Pays de la lavande*" it said in an ornate font, and on the back I recognized Gunnar's old-fashioned handwriting: "The scent is amazing. See you soon."

I pictured him alone in the house one afternoon, Marianne had gone shopping in another town, or caught the train to the Riviera with a girlfriend. I imagined Gunnar in the indolent afternoon sun of the South of France, the town with its stone houses and alleyways, little shops, a square with a few trees providing shade, a fruit stall, a fountain in the center. I saw him going to a tabac, buying a postcard and a stamp, then sitting down at an outdoor café and ordering a glass of pastis. Writing the card as he sipped his drink. Passing a mailbox on the way home before picking up some groceries for dinner. I wondered what he was thinking when he decided to send me the card, what he was thinking when he wrote it, whether "See you soon" was his way of saying that he missed me.

Sometimes I fantasized about traveling with him. Sitting next to him at the table in the square in the small French town, or elsewhere: in Germany, Greece, Italy. I had hardly been anywhere, I could count the countries I had visited on the fingers of one hand. Gunnar would be the perfect companion, he would be able to show me everything I ought to see. It was easy to picture us going to churches and museums together, looking at frescoes and ruins, enjoying a glass of wine in the shade in the afternoon, having dinner in a restaurant where the food was simple but delicious. He would tell me about the gods and thinkers of the ancient world, the artists and architects of the Renaissance, he would point out some detail in a church ceiling and make it seem utterly fascinating, the key to an understanding of something far more profound.

I saw him in my mind's eye, moved by history, by everything around us, created so long ago, preserved by human care for our collective past.

"People didn't appreciate the value of history until the Romantic period," I heard him say. "Before then, anything that preceded their own time and culture was seen as barbarian. During the Renaissance they removed stones from the Colosseum in order to build mansions in Rome."

"That seems pretty dumb, given how popular antiquity was during the Renaissance," I said.

He smiled. "Yes, that's definitely not a point in their favor," he said before giving the waiter a friendly wave and ordering another glass of wine.

The end of the evening was more difficult to imagine. Often I didn't get that far, it went against the grain, but sometimes I forced myself to continue my train of thought, saw us strolling together through the alleyways of an old town, far from home, the darkness compact and the air warm, suddenly we became aware of each other in a different way. The alleyway was narrow and smelled damp, enveloping us in a heavy atmosphere that made our conversation seem forced, left our words hanging in the air. We both wanted to linger in the moment, yet at the same time we wanted to hurry it along toward something else, something we couldn't articulate.

Were we walking close together? Did our shoulders touch occasionally, or our hands? Did we cross the hotel lobby together, hearing our footsteps echo on the tiles, did we pick up our keys from the concierge, did we stand side by side in the elevator, suddenly silent, our eyes darting around in embarrassment because we didn't know where to look? Did we say good night, thanks for today, and part company in the corridor? Did we go into our own rooms? Or the same room?

Sometimes I felt like a battery that was recharged by those Thursday afternoons, by everything he told me, everything we talked about, everything we established when it came to our view of the world. It made me tackle my job with fresh conviction, and gradually Gunnar's role at Rydéns and mine began to merge. It wasn't always entirely clear who was the publisher and who was the editor when it came to the books we worked on. In one instance I would be in charge, I was the one with the vision to create a fantastic novel from a mediocre manuscript, and he let me run with it, amused, with no desire to stake his claim. We would spend entire days in his office; I would take in my laptop in the morning, because there was always something we needed to sign off on or discuss, and I would stay there in one of the comfortable leather armchairs at the cluttered 1960s coffee table. It was always covered in piles of books, newspapers and international literary journals, printouts of manuscripts, a pretty ceramic bowl that was half-heartedly filled with fruit from time to time, but usually contained nothing but a few apples that were slowly shriveling. And then there were the increasingly unstable towers of the day's empty coffee cups, maybe the previous day's too, because we never got around to taking them to the lunchroom and putting them in the dishwasher.

Sitting there was special, particularly in the late afternoons during autumn and winter, when darkness fell quickly outside the window and the room felt like a cozy little grotto, wrapped in the green glow of the lamp. It made me feel safe and it smelled good, of coffee and paper and leather, warm, old-fashioned masculine scents. It must have smelled like this ever since Rydéns was built, and if I really tried I thought I could pick up a faint hint of tobacco, left over from the days when a great big ashtray would have sat in the middle of the table.

"You know," Gunnar said, "for years I've heard people compare publishing to panning for gold. You sit there up to your ears in unusable manuscripts, and occasionally a gold nugget pops up. As if it were a profession that principally depends on luck. It doesn't. It depends on how good you are at panning."

Together we were indisputably good at it. *Quiet Wind* wasn't the only one of our books to be nominated for a major prize. Several of them won, many sold well. Most attracted positive reviews, and Vilma Isaksson's second novel provoked a debate in the culture sections. At first the reviews were pretty lukewarm, but then came a second wave of columnists who questioned these reviews, arguing that they proved everything from the fact that literary criticism was in crisis, to the assertion that the individual in the postmodern condition was no longer capable of handling big stories.

Gunnar might seem unmoved by the attention, but I knew he was pleased because it made me happy. And it did, I felt as if Gunnar and I were creating contemporary literature, as if it were born and took shape at that messy coffee table in his office, and it was an intoxicating feeling.

I met quite a lot of men during those years, they showed up everywhere. It seemed to me that I was moving along in a way that I had never done before, and it hasn't happened since. At last I was an integral part of both the city and the world I had longed to be admitted to. I had the kind of self-confidence that comes from a following wind, the nights opened their arms to me. I went to parties where I had no idea if I would know anyone, and I always found someone to talk to. I went up to people and introduced myself, secure in the knowledge that they would want to talk to me, and they always did. I was considered beautiful back then, people in the industry knew who I was. I went to book launches and events and award ceremonies, I met others in the publishing world, along with authors, critics, writers who worked on the cultural pages. I often spoke to them about the kind of things Gunnar and I discussed, sometimes I heard myself repeating things he had said, making them my own.

It must have come across as strange, the fact that I was standing there with my shiny hair and high-heeled shoes expressing completely different views from the other young women who were around, surprisingly old-fashioned views on occasion. But the good thing about being a young woman is that everything can be turned into an advantage: Every word she says can be seen as both relevant and radical, because there are always plenty of people who, for ideological or financial reasons, think it is important to take young women's views seriously.

Because it's all about how things are said and who says them, rather than what is actually said. My views were interesting precisely because they were mine. If Gunnar had come out with them, they would have been regarded as obsolete, but now I was the one bringing them out one after the other, as if I were reaching into a curio cabinet full of rarely seen objects. This made some men uncomfortable, while others were delighted in spite of themselves. They were the ones I took home.

They always had the same names, the same looks. They were between thirty and forty, they often had a beard and wore a jacket, and maybe some kind of kudos in the world of cultural media. They were almost invariably mediocre lovers. It was just a matter of making my choice from a teeming market square full of bodies at my disposal, bodies to wake up next to, lying tired and slightly hungover beside each other in a stuffy apartment where neither of us had the energy to get up and make the coffee just yet.

I thought it was wonderful. Not only because of a lingering need for affirmation from times in my life when I had been too shy and unsure of myself ever to take the sexual initiative, but because I almost always experienced a brief and intense tenderness toward the person beside me. It had nothing to do with the sex, the tenderness was evoked by something else: a bad tattoo from their teenage years that bore witness to a completely different person from the one in bed with me now, a flash of insecurity in

the eyes of someone who always came across as supercon-
fident in public. A glimpse of vulnerability was the most
attractive thing I knew.

It was like a game, a series of field studies. What I
enjoyed most was the opportunity to compare the person
the morning after with the person from the night before,
to feel a sense of triumph at having been allowed behind a
facade, at having dug down to a truth. I thought it was all
beautiful, beautiful and fleeting.

I never really identified with the descriptions of the
mechanisms of dating that popped up in every other
manuscript submitted by young women. Now and then I
sensed those mechanisms, but perhaps I was spared. Perhaps I simply had the ability to understand people. If you
understand people, then everyone becomes interesting.

However open my heart might have been, it was always possible to open it a little more, open it wide like a
revolving door of tenderness for men to pass through, a
calm harbor of listening. I was always ready to caress the
back of their neck and say, "Tell me more," and they were
always ready to do just that.

Gunnar rarely went to parties or events, but he liked to
hear my accounts of those evenings. Who I had talked to
and what I thought of them, if I'd heard any interesting
gossip. I didn't usually mention how the evenings ended,
but I think he suspected anyway.

Sometimes I wondered about his interest in sex. I
thought he should have been able to get what he wanted

when he was younger, he must have found it easy to attract women with his quiet, gentlemanly ways, his ability to converse seamlessly, to make the other person feel seen and appreciated.

I once hinted that something had happened between me and one of the men at an event I'd attended, and Gunnar didn't seem particularly interested or uninterested, he responded with a distant politeness that left me feeling disappointed. I would have liked a different reaction, at least some hint of jealousy. Then it occurred to me that maybe he just didn't want to know because it was easier that way.

There are so many emotions for which we have no words. It's strange, but perhaps that's also because it's easier that way. We make sense of and organize our lives based on what we do have words for, just as we see colors based on the colors we know exist. The ancient Greeks had no word for "blue" as we understand it today, the words they used to describe the sea conveyed more than just the color: its texture, its opacity, its movement. In another language, or another age, Gunnar's and my relationship might have been different, maybe there would have been a word that encapsulated more than simply the one-dimensional "colleagues" and "friends."

As long as our association could be called friendship, then it was innocent according to the binary division of language, while a word edging toward attraction would have made things too complicated. At the same time, friendship often encompasses a measure of attraction, a hungry curiosity about the other person. What separates the strong feeling of a new friendship from falling in love can be nothing more than a linguistic formality. And emotions pay no heed to language. All those vague, homeless desires that hover between people every day like a quivering field of energy do not disappear because they don't have a name. They might even grow stronger for that very reason.

I don't think Gunnar was actually jealous because I sometimes went home with men after parties, but he obviously felt something, which he handled by wanting to know as little as possible. Similarly, it was better for me to know as little as possible about Marianne. He presumably understood that, because he rarely talked about her. I wondered if he told her about our afternoons at Bakfickan. She occasionally called him when we were sitting there, and he would answer tersely, his tone almost professional—no, he hadn't eaten, yes, he could pick up some groceries, see you later, bye. He seemed a little embarrassed that such a banal part of his life had crept into our world.

Our relationship was cut off from everything else, a bubble we had created together and in which we felt happy. We were a unit, he and I, as self-sufficient as an island. After several years at Rydéns I still hadn't joined my colleagues for one of their after-work gatherings. I knew these took place quite often, thanks to the plethora of emails from what was semi-ironically known as the Fun Committee. They arranged theater outings, bowling evenings, and post-work drinks. Gunnar never went along, so

I didn't either. I felt as if the whole thing had nothing to do with me, and as time went by I began to delete messages from the Fun Committee without even opening them.

Then Sally confronted me in the kitchen one afternoon and asked if I was unhappy, if there was something I wanted to talk about, and I realized that my colleagues were wondering why I never socialized with them. So I accepted an invitation for later that week, which involved everyone trooping off to an English pub a couple of blocks away for a burger and a few beers.

It was strange to see my colleagues in a new environment, where friendships and hierarchies were different from in the office. They talked about some of the bosses, but not Gunnar, and I got the sense that this was a conscious decision, because they knew that my loyalty lay with him. Maybe they thought I would gossip about them, and they were absolutely right. I sent him a few text messages during the course of the evening—Sally has talked about her dog Bobo four times, there's a lot of chat about who'll be allowed to go to Frankfurt—I adopted a slightly mocking tone, even though there wasn't really anything to mock. My colleagues were no dumber or sillier or more boring than colleagues generally are, no more irritating than people usually are. I'm sure I could have had a very pleasant evening if I'd been able to transfer my loyalty to them, just for a while.

When everyone had finished eating and settled around the table with a fresh round of drinks, I ended up next to Richard. He worked in the nonfiction department, and we'd never actually spoken before even though we'd seen each other in meetings and in the corridors and the lunchroom for years. It was embarrassing, especially when I noticed his familiar banter with everyone else. They all joked like friends do, as if they really meant something to one another. None of them meant anything to me, and of course I didn't mean anything to them, it was a straightforward but troubling realization. Apparently Tove and Andrea had shared an apartment in Italy on vacation, and everyone around the table was very much aware of Richard's interest in building conservation and gardening. We raised our glasses in a toast when he revealed that after waiting for many years, he had finally been given an allotment. It was all very congenial, but I couldn't ask him about it because I should have already known. I suddenly saw myself through my colleagues' eyes, and it was clear that I didn't fit in.

I tried to think of something to say to Richard, something that wasn't work-related or banal or too personal, but I couldn't think of anything, not a single thing, so I sat there in silence, smiling at the conversation around me, listening intently in the hope that I might be able to contribute a comment about something, anything, but the opportunity never arose. As the evening wore on I felt as self-conscious as when I was a teenager, as boring and out of place as during those first meetings at Rydéns.

When the party began to break up at about nine o'clock, some of us set off toward Slussen, and I found myself next to Richard again.

"Where are you headed?" he asked.

"Skanstull. How about you?"

"Gullmarsplan. I was thinking of walking. If you feel up to it we could keep each other company."

I had three unanswered texts from Gunnar, I had intended to reply on the way home, and I honestly wanted to get away from the lot of them. I'd thought that Richard wanted to get away from me too, because I hadn't exactly been sparkling company. Maybe he was asking out of politeness, hoping I would refuse.

"Okay," I said, mainly to test him.

It was a mild October evening, the sidewalks were covered in leaves, shimmering like a golden mosaic in the glow of the lights from the bars and restaurants on Götgatsbacken.

"I like what you do," Richard said.

More embarrassment—I didn't really know what he did. Was he the one behind that interview book with a former gang member? Or the book about weeds that became an unexpected success, selling to lots of countries? A famous US author had written an essay about it in *The New Yorker*.

"Thanks," I said.

"You have integrity."

This was getting worse by the minute. He'd noticed things about me.

"You have no idea what I do, right?" he said. "It's okay. Nothing exciting."

"No, I mean...sorry. The weed book?"

He laughed. "Yep, that was mine."

He was wearing a parka with a fur-lined hood that made him look like a member of a Britpop band, and the impression was heightened when he took out a packet of cigarettes and offered me one.

I shook my head.

"Do you mind if I..."

"No problem."

He smiled and lit his cigarette. "We have to allow ourselves at least one vice."

"Absolutely. I prefer alcohol."

"It's actually a terrible rhetoric, calling it a vice," he said. "As if life ought to consist only of what is necessary or beneficial."

"Nazism in its purest form," I said.

He laughed, glanced at me. "Why have you never come along to one of our after-work get-togethers before?"

It was an awkward question, and I didn't know what to say. I mumbled something about work taking up so much of my time anyway, which was a complete lie, and then I made a clumsy attempt to change the subject.

It struck me that I had always looked at Rydéns through Gunnar's eyes, which was why it had never occurred to me that anyone else there might be interesting or amusing, or even worth getting to know.

One night I had a dream about Gunnar. An erotic dream, more intense than any such dream before or since, yet at the same time it was almost chaste. I dreamed that we were sitting next to each other in Bakfickan one Thursday afternoon, that he put his hand on my thigh and kept it there.

That was all.

It was the most intense touch I had ever experienced, lingering in my mind like a fever long after I had woken up, like a secret room I could enter when I closed my eyes, a room thick with heavy, subdued excitement.

I didn't know how to deal with it. What had happened in my dream was surrounded by so many taboos that even daring to think about it seemed like a taboo. At the same time, the forbidden aspect made it even more of a turn-on.

I started to wonder whether Gunnar had ever imagined something similar about me. With hindsight it seems to me that he must have, that the idea must have occurred to him at least once, that he must have felt like I did when we parted company, a little tipsy after our Thursday wine, it would have been so easy to let our goodbye become a hug, to let that hug become something more.

Gunnar turned sixty-five at the end of May, and surprisingly he invited the entire fiction department to a party at the house in Gnesta. No doubt it was Marianne who suggested and planned the event, and on paper it sounded like a good idea. It was one of the first really sunny early-summer days, the lilacs were about to burst into flower, and nature was stunningly beautiful through the window of the commuter train.

The only photograph I have of Gunnar is from that afternoon. The five of us are standing there, Sally and Andrea and Peter and me, with Gunnar in the middle, all a little self-conscious in our finery, in clothes that aren't really warm enough for the season. My hair is ruffled by the wind and you can see that I am freezing, you can see that Gunnar isn't comfortable with the situation, possibly because two worlds are colliding: his wife, her sons, and their family friends, with acquaintances from the publishing industry and the team from Rydéns, two circles that never normally intersect. Our smiles are kind of stiff because of the unnatural situation, the chilly breeze, our stomachs are empty after our train journey because the buffet has not yet been laid out. The alcohol in the punch hasn't yet kicked in to lighten the atmosphere. There is an apple tree covered in blossoms behind us. It's a nice picture, but all I see when I look at the photograph now is Marianne holding the camera, calling out "Say cheese!" in a rather shrill voice. Above her the clouds are scudding across the sky as if they can sense the strained atmosphere and want to get away.

Maybe her presence contributed to Gunnar's fixed smile, maybe it didn't help that I was there, maybe it would have been easier for everyone if I'd turned down the invitation. But I really wanted to go, I wanted what we had to exist in reality, even if it was for only one afternoon and in a strained situation, where I was no more than one colleague among others.

I quickly downed several drinks and did my best to mingle with the other guests who had dispersed across the garden. I was finally able to put faces to the names I had heard often, both from Gunnar and others on the team: Leif, who had been an editor at Rydéns for many years, until his retirement, and Fredrik, who had worked closely with Gunnar as a publisher until a few years ago, when he had moved to one of the other major publishing houses.

Talking to them showed me what life might have looked like if things had been just a little different, if both of them had still been close colleagues of Gunnar's, if I hadn't happened to secure an internship at Rydéns, or if I hadn't stayed on, hadn't gotten to know Gunnar, and definitely hadn't attended his birthday party.

Fredrik wasn't much older than me, but he gave the impression of being very experienced, and I enjoyed talking to him. He told anecdotes that made all three of us laugh, about the time when a German author published by Rydéns came to Stockholm for an appearance that Fredrik was due to host. She was drunk when she got off the plane, and he and Gunnar spent several panic-stricken hours trying to get her in a fit state to face the public. Gunnar had walked her up and down Skeppsbron in the hope that the cold wind would enable her to pull herself together. I could picture him tucking his arm under hers and chatting pleasantly to her in his slightly stilted English, which I knew he didn't like to use. In the end she gave an impeccable performance.

Before Fredrik took his leave, he gave me his business card.

"It would be good to hear from you," he said.

No one had given me their card like that before, not unless there had been a specific reason for me to contact them. It was flattering, but it felt a little odd. I wasn't sure if it was some kind of networking reflex, or if there was a purpose behind it. I said exactly the same thing to Gunnar a while later when he asked if I was having a nice time, almost as if I were making a confession. If it was an attempt to lure me away from Rydéns, I wanted Gunnar to know about it, but he just smiled.

"It's always good to cultivate your contacts," he said. "Fredrik is a useful person to know, and a good publisher. I was sorry when he left Rydéns."

Then it was time for him to open his presents. The fiction department had chipped in to buy him a small oil painting that Andrea had found on an online auction site a few weeks earlier: late nineteenth century, artist unknown, a scene from Palermo, a city I knew Gunnar loved. It was a dark, romantic picture with beautifully dilapidated facades. As soon as I saw it I knew it was the perfect gift, and Gunnar seemed to feel the same. He looked genuinely touched and pleased when he took it out of the protective layers of cardboard and tissue paper and gazed at it.

I thought maybe it wouldn't fit in so well in the house, the decor was colorful and middle-class, but he had a study where he could no doubt find a suitable place to hang it. I had glanced inside on passing, the walls were covered with bookshelves interspersed with paintings, just like his office at Rydéns. There was a big old-fashioned linen press just by the door, and on it stood a large crystal bowl next to a black-and-white photograph of Gunnar as a little boy, together with his mother and an old cork float. The little still life gave an almost sacred impression in spite of its worldliness, like a shrine to something that was lost. I made a mental note to ask him about the float.

It was always understood that Gunnar would carry on working after sixty-five, but then his heart began to act up. During the following autumn he had several twinges, in the spring he was taken to the hospital for observation, but was sent home. Every time I felt sick with worry, I went around in a fog of paralyzing fear until he sent a reassuring text message: Everything was fine, he would soon be back at work.

Maybe it was Marianne who kept telling him to slow down and spend a greater proportion of the year in France. That was the plan, he explained at one of our Monday meetings, and it was going to happen very soon. With just a few weeks' notice he was going down to part-time, no more than fifty percent of his current workload. He would arrange things to suit him, and would primarily work remotely.

I was hurt that he had made these plans with Marianne without even mentioning them to me before making the announcement to everyone on the team, and the thought of him simply disappearing was brutal. Our last Thursday afternoon at Bakfickan before the summer was painful, I felt both let down and sad. Everything we had achieved over several years at Rydéns we had done together, and now I would be left alone. I suspected that our contact would become increasingly sporadic, more and more about work-related matters, less about us. I began to cry quietly when he asked for the bill, he noticed but didn't know how to handle it, he cleared his throat and mumbled a few awkward, meaningless phrases in order to avoid what really ought to be said. He often did that.

"Of course we'll still see each other," he assured me when we said goodbye. "I'll still be in town for some of the week."

I nodded through my tears and I think he was about to give me a hug, but he changed his mind, as if he had stopped himself at the last second from doing something inappropriate. So I did it instead: I threw my arms around him and pulled him close, laid my cheek against his rough coat and inhaled the discreet fragrance I had smelled from a distance every day since I started at Rydéns. After a few seconds he hugged me back, tightly and briefly. He looked at me with an expression I hadn't seen before, serious and tender at the same time, then he turned and set off down Fredsgatan.

It had been impossible to imagine the publishing house without him. In so many ways he *was* Rydéns, he was its soul, he was the one who knew its history, who knew everything about the list and the authors and colleagues over the years. I had expected him to show up at regular intervals to make sure that we were behaving ourselves, that his hand and spirit would hover over both the list and our daily work for a long time to come.

But everything continued without him. No one, absolutely no one is irreplaceable, which is a depressing realization. A workplace is like a microcosm of nature, ruled by the laws of evolution: As one species dies out and the whole system is destabilized, an efficient mechanism kicks in to ensure the survival of everyone else, and before long there is a new system, a new balance. Nature's sole purpose is survival, and the same is true of capitalism: A company is like a self-generating animal, a starfish that grows a new arm if a new arm is needed.

I remembered a conversation with Gunnar in Bakfickan, when I had referred to "the survival of the strongest," and he had pointed that the Swedish version was in fact a mistranslation.

"Darwin wrote about 'the survival of the fittest.' That doesn't mean the strongest survive, but those who are the best at adapting to the prevailing circumstances."

"Survival of the pathetic," I muttered. I was upset about something and for once he was the one calming me down.

"Sometimes you have to adapt," he said.

I certainly had to adapt.

Jenny was taking over some of Gunnar's responsibilities in a newly created post where she shared the title of editor in chief with him. However, she was also tasked with conducting a more open dialogue with both the finance and marketing departments than Gunnar had. She announced the changes at one of our Monday meetings, looking very important, then embarked on a PowerPoint presentation outlining how she planned to restructure the way we worked. The relatively free rein we had been given by Gunnar would be tightened, the reporting of every single decision was essential, and everything had to go through Jenny.

This also applied to Gunnar, and when he realized that he would have to report to Jenny, he informed the company that he had changed his mind about working part-time and would instead be leaving Rydéns and retiring, effective immediately.

And so he disappeared from public life, like so many men of his generation had before him. It was an era when this wasn't regarded as unfortunate, there were more aging white men in positions of power than were needed, it was high time they stepped aside so that others could fill their posts and make the world a fairer, more reasonable place.

I often thought about how incredibly shortsighted contemporary society was, about how everything Gunnar had taught me was on a completely different level from what anyone of my own generation had to offer. Those who were supposed to represent the cultural establishment of the future preferred to think rather than act, their conversation was littered with banal signal words, and they engaged opportunistically with whatever trivial issues might be trending. None of them was capable of creating something like the Andromeda imprint—not that any of them would want to.

We kept in touch, Gunnar and I, he texted me several times a week, but his messages changed pretty quickly after he left Rydéns. The anger within him, which I had always regarded as a consequence of his high ideals, was now turned up a notch and became more blunt and vulgar. He complained about the old bitches writing for the cultural sections in the press, the PC critics, and the fucking number crunchers at the publishing houses who got to make all the decisions even though they were fucking worthless.

I began to suspect that he had drunk his half bottle of wine even though it wasn't Thursday, and maybe a few more glasses on top of that, before he called me. He seemed to grab the chance to pick up the phone if he was out on an errand, or if Marianne wasn't home.

"Have you seen what that fucker's written now?" he would bellow, assuming that I knew what he was talking about. And I usually did. It was almost always the editor of some culture section or one of the leading critics who had done something that in Gunnar's eyes was unforgivable.

As time went by I grew tired of the whole rigmarole, him telling me stories I'd heard before, his increasing anger toward everything associated with the establishment or commercialism. I became particularly uncomfortable when he directed his disappointment at me. Now that he was no longer a part of Rydéns, the company couldn't do anything right as far as Gunnar was concerned. I was allocated the role of both infiltrator and enemy, although I could tell that he was trying to keep himself in check when it came to the latter. He didn't always succeed, and then I was the one that took the brunt of his anger over what he saw as ridiculous decisions. When I told him that Jenny had given me a famous actor's debut novel to work on, he reacted as if I had sold my soul to the devil.

"How can you lower yourself to deal with crap like that?" he yelled when he called me one afternoon. I had to go downstairs and out into the street to be able to talk to him in private.

"You were the one who told me you have to compromise sometimes," I said with hot tears springing to my eyes, but he wasn't really listening. I thought he was being unfair, I was on his side, after all. I was more on his side than anyone else.

Meanwhile I started to realize how sheltered my working life had been under Gunnar. One day Jenny called me into her office to discuss my time reporting, which came as a surprise as I had never logged my hours during all the years I'd spent at Rydéns. I had assumed I was on flexible working hours, and I stuck to them conscientiously except for the afternoons at Bakfickan. However, I felt that I more than compensated for those with all the unpaid reading I did at home.

Whenever Gunnar used to complain about Jenny, I had assumed it was a sign of an old-fashioned and pretty innocent lack of experience in having a female boss. He revered women in general, sometimes in a way that wasn't entirely unproblematic from a contemporary viewpoint, and I knew that his gentlemanly appreciation was based on an enormous respect for independent women who worked hard. He actually judged women by the same criteria as men—rigorously—but for a man of his age it didn't matter how consistent he was, because any issues with taking orders from a woman would always be seen as a greater infraction than issues with taking orders from a man.

Jenny was obviously pleased that Gunnar wasn't around anymore, and everyone in the department who wanted to remain in her good graces silently espoused her attitude.

Suddenly it was as if I had been hurled back to those early days at Rydéns, as if my colleagues were wondering what I was doing there, as if the prize nominations and sales figures counted for next to nothing against the fact that I hadn't logged my hours.

It was an incredibly humiliating meeting, with Jenny saying in a somewhat condescending tone, "In this establishment we believe that everyone should follow the same rules," and I left feeling angry with both her and Gunnar. Had it never occurred to him how it would look if I were some kind of unspoken exception to the rules that applied to every other employee? I had never liked Jenny, she was a careerist with a strange lack of independence, even though she managed to make it seem that the opposite was true. She also had no real vision, which was remarkable for someone who liked to pontificate about the future.

I would have liked to call Gunnar and tell him exactly that, align myself with his view that Rydéns was going downhill. But he was the one who had put me in this position, albeit with the best of intentions. I felt alone.

For the past few years my life had centered almost entirely on Gunnar, and without him the evenings and weekends began to seem very empty. I wasn't looking forward to the summer, even though we had never seen each other during the holidays. It had been manageable because we had kept in touch when projects we were working on continued through the summer, giving me a reason to contact him about final edits and proofs. It had given me the sense that he was still there, even if he wasn't available just then.

One evening when my phone buzzed with a text I assumed it was Gunnar, but in fact it was Richard, wondering what I was doing. He was in my neighborhood, would I maybe like to meet him for a drink? I felt almost disloyal, as if I were going behind Gunnar's back in even considering it, as if I ought to text him right away and tell him, "You'll never guess what just happened! Richard from nonfiction asked me out for a drink," then wait for his reaction.

But I didn't. I went out into the spring evening, I walked along the ugliest section of Götgatan and thought it was beautiful, shimmering with promise, and Richard was standing outside the bar in his parka smoking a cigarette, and for the first time it struck me how attractive he was. It was as if a barrier had given way in my head, a sluice gate had opened allowing desire to surge through with a force that surprised me. I didn't want to sit and chat and have a drink with Richard, I wanted to take him by the hand and go back to my apartment and have sex with him, slowly and deliberately, and the thought made me smile at him and he smiled back in a way that made me wonder if he could read my mind, if he could see straight into me and liked what he saw.

Needless to say I couldn't talk to him like I used to talk to Gunnar. Our worldviews were too different, not to mention our opinions on literature. Richard had no great ambitions to work on something life-changing, something that would leave its mark on history. He regarded what he did as a job, nothing more and nothing less. At first that disappointed me, and I thought it was typical: He was one of those who didn't get it, who'd wormed their way into an industry that should be run by people with passion, people who understood the essential nature of literature.

Instead he was contented. He was happy with his job, and above all with having a steady, decent income. He didn't think there was much to complain about in the world of literature in general or in contemporary literature, and in any case he was more au fait in nonfiction. He was happy with his book about weeds, not necessarily because he was particularly interested in weeds but because it had sold well and attracted critical attention. It had earned him a certain measure of respect at Rydéns and counted as an important step in his career.

Then I began to feel that it might be a healthy attitude. A little bit boring and definitely not romantic, but
not necessarily reprehensible. It was fun to have someone
to do things with, someone who was accessible in a way
that felt like a luxury, our time together was not beset
by terms and conditions. We met one Friday evening
for dinner, then ended up spending the whole weekend
together. Which wasn't especially remarkable, I guess
that's what happens in the early stages of a relationship,
but for me the mere fact that Richard wanted to be with
me was enough of a reason to want to see him again the
following weekend. We also saw each other on a few
evenings during the week, evenings that ended with him
spending the night at my apartment and going to work in
the same clothes as the previous day. He left before me
in the mornings so that we wouldn't arrive at the office
together, and for the rest of the day we would exchange
delighted glances in the corridors, touch briefly at the
coffee machine if there was no one else in the lunchroom, text each other with the suggestion that we should
sneak off to an empty conference room.

One weekend he took me to his allotment, high up on
a hill in the south of Tantolunden, with an amazing view
of the waters of Årstaviken sparkling in the sun. It was a
beautiful place, an uneven, steep plot with mature fruit
trees and beds, a paved seating area, a little red hut with
mullioned windows and two small rooms.

"It's almost impossible to get an allotment up here
these days," Richard explained. "The waiting time is

ridiculous. But Grandma put me on the list when I was little—I was already into gardening back then."

He gave a smile that was a mixture of pride and embarrassment. Then he showed me around, told me about the spring flowers that were everywhere, drifts of daffodils, narcissi, and extraordinary tulips that looked as if exotic birds had landed among his beds. He worked for a few hours while I sat in the sun reading, and then I helped him water the newly planted peonies and autumn anemones. As twilight fell, we wrapped ourselves in blankets and drank prosecco, a string of lights came on in the old apple tree, the buildings on the quayside at Liljeholm cast their shining reflection on the dark water, and trains passed across the Årsta Bridge like long, glowing worms.

There was an uncomfortable sofa bed in the hut, and before we fell asleep we lay close to each other in the darkness and talked. In fact he did most of the talking, telling me that his father had wanted Richard to pursue an academic career like he had, or at least opt for a better profession than publisher, which to my ears sounded like an insult to both of us. I also thought this was a problem for a person who doesn't actually have any major problems, but I was touched that he wanted to tell me about it, and it was clearly important to him.

"Tell me more," I said, stroking the back of his neck, and like everyone else, he wanted to do just that.

We slept late the next morning, and when we were woken by the bright spring sun that had found its way in through the inadequate blinds, there were three new texts from Gunnar on my phone. He was going to be in the city that afternoon and wondered if I wanted to meet. The messages had a demanding tone that made me feel ill at ease. It was as if they came from a different world, a completely different existence, and the thought of informing Richard that I was going off to meet Gunnar was problematic. It would also ruin our plans to cook together later.

When I told him, he muttered "Oh, okay," in a resigned tone of voice that annoyed me. We weren't even a couple, I thought, we just saw each other occasionally, there was no reason for him to get annoyed with me. And at the same time I was annoyed with Gunnar because it was his fault that I had annoyed Richard. It was typical of him to contact me this weekend when I had plans for once, and enjoyable plans at that. Walking through Kungsträdgården toward Bakfickan, I felt annoyed with everything.

Something had happened to Gunnar's face since I last saw him. It was sunken, with gray shadows, his skin had a greenish tinge, as if it were lit by cold, unpleasant moonlight. I have never liked moonlight; there is something creepily parasitic about it, a cold, secondhand light, an eerie reflection of the day's warm sunlight. Like when you look at a photo negative and try to imagine the finished picture, but you can't see past the fact that the faces are stiff and resemble wax models, you can sense the skull biding its time beneath the skin.

That was what Gunnar looked like now. He suddenly had an old man's face, and I found it hard to think about anything else, to relax and engage in our conversation. It wasn't the same as before. Our gossip about work colleagues had always had a tender undertone, but that was gone. He sounded harsh, almost scornful. Maybe he had arrived early, sat in the bar drinking alone for a while, because his gaze, which had always been sharp, was somehow hazy, unfocused.

It was naïve of me, but that was the first time I realized that Gunnar was going to die.

It only took a few months. I arrived at work and saw that the flag was flying at half-mast, and at first I didn't understand, I assumed that one of our colleagues who was really old must have died. And then I became aware that lots of people had found out before me. Marianne had contacted Jenny, Jenny had contacted the janitor and asked him to sort out the flag before anyone said anything to me. Everyone gathered in the lunchroom already knew. Andrea's eyes shone with unshed tears and she said, "Have you heard? It's Gunnar," and it was wrong, it was all wrong, I should have been the one telling them.

And it was all wrong when Richard came to console me. He knew that Gunnar and I had worked closely together and had gone out for a drink occasionally, and actually there was nothing more to tell, that was exactly what our relationship had looked like. Perhaps it wasn't surprising that he was taken aback by my devastation, by the fact that my grief was not subdued but raging, as if Gunnar's death were a personal injustice against me, and yet that was how I felt. I was angry with everyone, I blamed everyone. Richard's arms around me were heavy and challenging: Grieve in a way that enables me to console you, they said, grieve in a way that unites us against your sorrow. But I didn't want to be united with him, the person with whom I had been united was gone, and Richard's arms defiled the memory of that union. I felt nauseated, suffocated, I had to break free, and I thought Richard looked ridiculous, sitting there with his simple, sad face, I thought he was just generally too simple.

Gunnar's death prompted a small news item in the publishing industry press, and a few short pieces on the culture pages. They were very matter-of-fact, brief biographies with a mention of some of his better-known authors. "After a lengthy illness," they said; that was wrong too, it made him sound like a frail old man, as if he had died in a hospital bed, as if his death had been expected for a long time. And the following day the newspapers were thrown away, the epitaph on the Rydéns website had disappeared beneath the flood of posts about the success of a series of crime novels and a debut author's appearance on a TV program. The news about death was over, but death itself continued.

How do you mourn a relationship like that? A relationship that had been more real than any other in my life, but had never actually existed in reality, never manifested itself in public, never been designated by a term that encapsulated its true nature. There was no one I could share my grief with, because those who mourned him as I did had no idea that I mourned like them, nor should they find out. Maybe we are always alone in our grief, but not quite so alone, not weighed down beneath a secret that turned into shame inside my head at the thought of seeing Marianne at the funeral, and the shame turned into anger at the thought of having to go up to her and possibly take her hand, say that I was sorry for her loss, when she ought to be saying the same thing to me.

The person I was with him had died, our mutual understanding of the world was gone, the whole world seen through our eyes was lost. And the worst thing of all was the lack of closure. I had left our last meeting feeling somehow disappointed, both because I was annoyed with him and because the fact that he had become a different person seemed like a betrayal. Over and over again I thought about how it should have been, how I should have looked him in the eyes and finally said all those things I ought to have said long ago: You taught me everything, thank you for believing in me like no one had believed in me before, thank you for the person I became because of you, thank you for allowing me to become a person who knows someone like you.

What was I without him? Now I was only me.

It rained on the day he was buried. I spent an eternity in the florist's the previous evening trying to choose a flower to lay on his coffin, and the longer I stood there, the harder it got. In the end it felt as if my choice of flower would be the final distillation of what our relationship had meant to me, my very last chance to do right by him. But all the flowers struck me as terribly banal, unworthy of a man like him. How could I place on his coffin a boring rose from a boring florist's shop next to a boring staircase leading down to a boring subway station? I found the roses ugly, almost repulsive, I needed something else, something elevated, something more beautiful. Unfortunately there was nothing more beautiful on sale, and I got angry with everything—with the florist, with the society that didn't demand flowers more worthy than banal roses by the dozen, with myself because I couldn't even do something as simple as buying a flower—and I began to weep silently in front of the glass cabinet containing the ugly flowers in their ugly buckets.

Every day of our lives when we don't have to be confronted with death is a blessing, I said to myself, and then it occurred to me that it sounded like something out of a self-help book, that my words were as banal as the roses. When we are faced with death everything becomes banal, and that realization was also banal, everything was banal and the rose I bought was ugly and Gunnar was dead, he would go on being dead, he would be dead forever.

Marianne and her sons were seated right at the front of the church, along with the sons' wives or girlfriends, people who hadn't known Gunnar the way I'd known him, while I was consigned to the "colleagues" category, and what was Jenny doing there anyway, how dare she even look sad.

I hardly remember the wake, but a lot of people were there. I recognized a few from Gunnar's sixty-fifth birthday party: Leif and Fredrik, whom I'd spoken to back then, while others were older, acquaintances from the world of publishing, the men from the same generation that he used to meet for lunch. Representatives from a higher sphere were also in attendance: former editors in chief of publishing houses, newspaper owners and editors, many of them considerably older than Gunnar. It made me angry to see them standing there, it wasn't fair that they were still alive while Gunnar was dead, and the boring food made me angry, as did the plain coffee mugs provided by the community center. We carve a bizarre frame for life's greatest mystery, we let banality keep it in place.

Maybe it's a way of controlling the whole thing, I thought, and suddenly it became clear to me that that was how it had to be, that Gunnar wouldn't have wanted it any other way. There was an ordinariness about the situation that was a part of his inheritance, in the chipped mugs, the Duralex glasses, the half-hearted little bunches of carnations placed along the well-used linen tablecloths. I remembered what he had told me about his childhood, about his mother, he once said that the stone walls you see everywhere dividing Swedish fields and meadows were a part of his history. For generations people like his relatives had spent their time digging stones out of the ground in order to make the land usable for farming, they had carefully stacked them on top of one another around the fields, and the walls they built are still standing today.

It was an important image as far as he was concerned: His forefathers hadn't built cities or cathedrals, they hadn't given rise to articles in newspapers or biographical dictionaries, but they had left their mark on the landscape, humble monuments to a lost age.

And I realized that there was nothing wrong with the ordinariness of his funeral and wake, in fact it was beautiful and dignified.

For a long time I was haunted by the feeling that it couldn't just end. I don't know what I was waiting for, maybe a call from Marianne telling me that he'd left me something. I pictured her going through his study and finding an item he'd wanted me to have, a letter, a wish that one of the books from his enormous collection should be passed on to me. One day there would be an envelope on my desk that would somehow put things right, at least partly. That would bring closure.

But it didn't happen. I tried to console myself with the thought that he'd died suddenly, so maybe that was why, but it made me sad. What if there was unfinished business on his side too, what if there was something he'd wanted to say but never gotten around to it? Maybe things could have ended very differently if I'd only answered his calls more often toward the end, put up with his predictable diatribes, with hearing him talk contemptuously about things that I actually despised too but had to tolerate because that was my job. What if he had been disappointed in me when he died?

Over and over again I thought back to how we parted company on those Thursday evenings, how we stood between the Royal Opera House and Saint Jakob's Church, and he was probably in a hurry to catch his train but was enough of a gentleman not to rush our goodbyes, he would rather walk more quickly on his way to the station. In the autumn and winter it was already dark, the moment always felt charged, we were both a little tipsy and it was as if all our emotions were heightened thanks to the wine, the deepening twilight, the intimate hours we had just shared in the restaurant. It is a place in the middle of the city that feels like a back street, a place where something could have happened—that was how it always seemed to me, but nothing ever did happen. He would thank me for my company, wish me a nice weekend, nothing more. "You too," I would say. Then he would disappear in the direction of Fredsgatan.

The atmosphere at Rydéns changed after Gunnar's death. He was a completed chapter now, and Jenny was determined to rip up the remaining elements of his influence and make a fresh start. One morning we were informed that everyone in the office was to change places immediately, and we obeyed in grim silence, like a group of schoolchildren. We packed up our belongings and waited for the guys from IT to come and move our computers, even though the reorganization was ill-thought-out and would make our work considerably less efficient. It was clear that the aim was not to improve our situation but was a decision taken by a boss who wanted to demonstrate her power by forcing everyone to do something pointless. At the same time it was highly significant, no doubt introduced in the hope of smashing old structures and loyalties.

At a meeting one afternoon, a manuscript that had been accepted for the Andromeda imprint came up for discussion.

"How are we going to handle this?" Jenny said, glancing around the table.

"I'll take it," I said.

I didn't really understand why the question had arisen; I was the only one who had worked on Andromeda.

Jenny frowned slightly. "We've decided to pause Andromeda."

"What do you mean?"

"I mean exactly what I said. We need to take a look at the format."

"The format?"

She cleared her throat. "To be honest, we need to take a look at everything. The authors, the style of the books, the whole concept. It feels...old-fashioned. People no longer care whether a book is part of an imprint, a series, they don't need anyone else to choose for them. They're used to making their own choices. The focus group had some very interesting input."

"The focus group?"

I recalled Jenny mentioning a focus group in a meeting some years ago; Gunnar had dismissed the idea.

"So you want to bring in a bunch of students and make sure they say exactly what the number crunchers want to hear, in exchange for a cup of coffee and a ticket to the movies?" he'd said. Jenny had mumbled some evasive answer but had clearly taken it further, all the way to letting a group of strangers decide what became of his life's work.

My head was pounding. I thought about what Gunnar had told me on one of those afternoons at Bakfickan: He wanted me to take over. I was the one who must move Andromeda forward. He would make sure it happened. And even if I'd never dared to believe that it would actually come about, or that I would be able to shoulder everything he had built up, the thought had lingered in the back of my mind. Andromeda should be administered by me, because I was the only one who understood what that involved.

"But…" I began, "Gunnar said…"

Everyone was looking at me. I felt like a child, complaining about a perceived injustice.

"Gunnar is no longer in charge here," Jenny snapped. "So you need to speak to the author. Explain the situation, tell her we're pausing the series while we reevaluate it, but that of course we will honor our side of the agreement and publish the book. As an ordinary novel. You can work on it, but in the future I think we need to take a look at your assignments too."

Blank expressions all around the table. No one would meet my gaze, but I knew exactly what they were thinking: From now on, the same rules apply to you as to everyone else.

"What did Jenny actually have against Gunnar?" I asked Andrea one day when we were sitting in the lunchroom with our uninspiring salads in front of us.

"Well, of course things got a little tense after the ... incident," she said.

"Incident? What incident?"

She looked at me suspiciously. "Didn't you hear about it? I thought everyone knew. It was back in the nineties, some PR girl who worked here for a while. She's at Hammarlund now. She and Jenny are old friends. To be honest I don't know exactly what happened, but apparently she and Gunnar used to flirt with each other, and he somehow crossed the line."

"What? That doesn't sound like Gunnar at all! Are you sure? Did Jenny tell you this?"

She didn't answer my questions. Instead she said, "They used to go to a bar after work and sit there chatting. It seems to have been ... well, just like it was with you and Gunnar."

She kept her eyes fixed on mine, and I got the feeling that she'd been waiting to say this for a very long time.

"What do you mean?" I replied, although of course I knew what she was getting at.

"Oh, come on—you might as well be honest. No one thinks you don't deserve your position here anymore, but you have to admit that it was strange that you got it in the first place."

"Strange? In what way?" I asked stupidly.

"You were an intern, and you were appointed overnight. You got a job that usually requires both a qualification and a lot more experience than you had. There were others who wanted that job, let me tell you."

"Seriously? You think I got the job because..."

"Because you and Gunnar were in a relationship, yes."

She shoved the last few spinach leaves into her mouth, stood up, and threw the empty salad box in the trash can.

I stayed where I was, my head burning with a vague shame that slowly turned into anger, a feverish sense of in- justice. I hadn't done anything wrong. I had been fortunate enough to say the right things to Gunnar in the beginning, but they could easily have been the wrong things if I'd said them to someone else, which would have meant no offer to extend my internship, and I would have thrown away my chance to establish myself in the world of publishing. I hadn't secured any advantages by flirting, I hadn't used anyone or been used, and I wanted to run after Andrea and tell her how wrong she was, how wrong everyone was, but any attempt to do so would be seen as proof of the polar opposite—that my loyalty did indeed lie with Gunnar.

In the past I had never felt any reluctance to go to work in the morning, quite the reverse. Any trace of Sunday- evening angst had disappeared as soon as I found my feet and began to enjoy life at Rydéns. In fact I had almost missed the place over the weekends, missed seeing Gun- nar. Now the opposite was true. Waking up in the morn- ing was hard, waking up to the depressing realization that everything just kept on going. How could the world just keep on going? *Someone is missing*, I wanted to shout, *we can't just carry on as usual when someone is missing.* And how could the work at Rydéns simply continue? If there was one place where it should be obvious at every single moment that Gunnar was gone, it was Rydéns.

But the catalog introducing the season's new books was launched as usual. The Fun Committee organized after-work drinks. I ignored the first email, and when a reminder dropped into my in-box, I deleted it. I couldn't hang out with the others anymore. It would be a betrayal of Gunnar, a betrayal of everything we had been together. And a betrayal of myself. How could I sit there trying to enjoy myself when I knew what they were saying about me, when I knew what they thought they knew?

"Are you coming tonight?" Sally asked as we were gathered in a conference room waiting for Jenny to start the daily meeting.

"I don't think I've got time," I mumbled.

Richard gave me a look that meant I felt nothing but contempt for him. I saw him through Gunnar's eyes: mediocre, an opportunist. He doesn't understand what literature is, I thought. He isn't an intellectual person.

And so the spring party came around, also without Gunnar. At first I wasn't going to go, because the thought of standing there on the roof without him was too upsetting. But then I decided that I ought to do what Gunnar would have done, what a gentleman would do in a situation like this. The dignified thing was to go, to look after our authors, make sure they had an enjoyable evening. Plus the weather was perfect, Gunnar would have appreciated that. It was late May, there was a faint haze in the air that softened the otherwise harsh spring sunshine and made it feel pleasant, the horizon was a distant blue blur, like in a Renaissance painting.

The older authors arrived first as usual, gathering in a group where everyone knew one another, pleased to renew their acquaintance. I didn't feel brave enough to approach them on my own, but after a while Amelie Stjärne came over to me.

"I was so sorry to hear about Gunnar," she said. "I know he meant a lot to you. He meant a lot to me too, but the two of you must have been very close."

"Thank you—we were. We worked together for years and...and..."

I didn't know how to go on. She looked at me with kindness in her eyes, and for the first time I had the feeling that someone actually understood.

"They don't make them like Gunnar anymore," she said, gently placing her hand on my arm. "Which is also sad. It won't be the same here without him."

"No. No, it definitely won't."

Sally joined us and began to enthuse about Amelie's latest book. I went to the bar for a glass of wine. The buffet was still well-stocked, so I picked up a plate and chose a few canapés, asked the bartender for a glass of white. He placed it on the counter in front of me with a metallic clink.

There weren't many people at the bar yet, I looked all the way along it, but apart from a few glasses it was empty. No coasters in sight. They were usually piled up like little towers, the bartender would reach for the top one and with a smooth, practiced movement would slide it under the glass, completing the experience of being at Rydéns, of being a part of something bigger than the present. Being a part of history.

"Where are the coasters?" I asked the bartender.

"Sorry?"

"Aren't there any coasters? To put the glasses on?"

"Not as far as I know."

Jenny was standing by the railing talking to a woman I recognized but couldn't quite place, she was well made-up in a way that almost looked airbrushed, presumably she was one of the commercial authors whose names I never managed to learn. I went over to them.

"Excuse me Jenny, but…"

My expression made it clear that I had something important on my mind, she excused herself, moved to one side, and nodded at me.

"They've forgotten the coasters," I said.

She stared at me blankly. She obviously didn't have a clue what I was talking about.

"The coasters to put the glasses on," I clarified. "There are no coasters on the bar."

"Sofie," she said quietly, "we decided to stop using the coasters. If I remember correctly, you were at the meeting where we discussed our new green policy?"

"What?" I said a little too loudly, she glared at me.

"We'll talk about this tomorrow," she said, then she turned back to her companion with a big smile. "I do apologize," I heard her say in her warmest tone of voice. "Where were we?"

They had destroyed everything that meant something. They had dumped everything that had gone before and continued to move forward without a care in the world, and the worst thing of all was that they could do that. Everyone got used to the new way very quickly, and before long they all thought the current state of affairs was so much better.

Entire worlds disappear every day. Entire systems of memories and relationships are obliterated, then everything simply continues. Gunnar would soon be forgotten, even here at Rydéns, in the place to which he had given his whole life, the place he had created, in many ways. Now his authors were aging and his imprint was old-fashioned, in the corridors people talked about him like an old man with a dubious attitude toward women, his office had been emptied, all his books and paintings were gone, along with the green lamp and the cluttered coffee table, and the head of the new audiobook department was sitting there instead of Gunnar. A whole life efficiently cleared away, because times had changed and everyone chose to change along with them.

I heard Gunnar's gentle voice in my head as I stood there with the spring evening before me, the dizzying view

THERESE BOHMAN

and the copper rooftops with their beautiful patina, glowing green in the twilight, I heard him say that nostalgia has been turned into a taboo. I understood exactly what he meant. The feeling that everything is slipping through your fingers, the deeply existential sorrow at the futility of trying to stop it, the bitterness of being alone in that realization. Gunnar was a part of my history, and now he was gone. I heard him say that we should take care of the small amount of history we have. "Especially people like us," he said on one of those afternoons at Bakfickan, his gaze holding mine over the rim of his wineglass.

As well as the literature he created, I thought, he created me.

Tucked inside my wallet was the business card I had been given at Gunnar's sixty-fifth birthday party by his former colleague, who had said it would be good to hear from me. I had thought about it in passing once or twice, but had never even considered making the call. I took it out. It was a little dog-eared, but legible: Fredrik Widell, Publisher.

I finished off the last of my wine, then got out my phone and firmly keyed in the numbers, buoyed by my resolve. He answered almost immediately.

"Oh hi," I said. "It's Sofie Andersson from Rydéns—we met at Gunnar Abrahamsson's birthday party, and... and at his funeral, unfortunately."

"Of course," he said. His tone was warm, friendly. "Hi Sofie."

"You told me to give you a call," I said. "So... that's what I'm doing."

He laughed. "I hoped you would. How are things at Rydéns?"

"It's not the same."

"I can imagine." He lowered his voice, suddenly sounding confidential. "I'm actually in the process of starting up something that I think might interest you. Both of us have worked with Gunnar, so we probably have roughly the same view on the direction it might take. He always sang your praises."

Behind me people were laughing, I no longer cared about them, I no longer cared about the party. It was soulless and meaningless, an event for those who were happy to go along with the prevailing conditions at Rydéns, publishers and editors who were worried about their jobs and were prepared to adapt, authors who would happily drink their free wine and smile at everyone as long as their books were published and their small advances paid.

"Tell me more," I said.

"You could say it's not too dissimilar to Andromeda, so I really believe you could make a valuable contribution," he said. "I'd be delighted to talk you through my ideas, but it would be better if we could meet up."

"Let's do that," I replied. "Let's have lunch."

"Absolutely—this week? Do you have anywhere in mind?"

"I know a very good place," I said.

2.

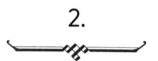

IT'S FUNNY HOW there seems to be a perception of a time gone by when things were better organized than they are now: there were fewer divorces, the nuclear family was stronger, people were healthier and more trustworthy and perhaps a little dull, and society in general was less complicated.

If you scratch the surface, it often reveals a mess. It is possible to find illegitimate and adopted children in almost every family, someone who grew up with their aunt or grandmother instead of with their parents, someone suffering with their nerves or mental health issues, someone who went out into the barn and hanged themselves. No one talked about emotions, that kind of thing just happened. It was part of life, dealt with pragmatically but never discussed.

My mother's family were farmers from Söderman-land. She moved to Stockholm in her late teens to seek her fortune in the big city, like so many before her. She loved to go out dancing, played music at home, and smoked the odd cigarette. At the same time she was anything but bohemian, she carried the inheritance of the days when Sweden was a poverty-stricken country, the difficulties of the Second World War, growing up on a farm where you could never take anything for granted. One of the strongest memories from my childhood is the refrigerator: Nothing could be thrown away. I can still see a few leftover boiled potatoes on a saucer, some meatballs, a drop of cream in a glass, anything that could be fried or added to a stew or an omelet. She liked omelets, she thought they were sophisticated, French. She had never been abroad.

In Stockholm she took a series of casual jobs before finding a permanent post with the Customs Service. It was pure chance, like so many things back then, in a time when self-realization didn't exist and no one was expected to be passionate about their job. She was happy there, perhaps mainly because she was working in an office. Her tasks may have been straightforward and monotonous, but they were a world away from the heavy work on the farm in Södermanland or the factory jobs she had done.

She never spoke about dreams. She wasn't physically tired in the evenings, she could have dreamed, but people didn't do that. Life was here and now, and she was glad she didn't have to worry about the weather and the harvest. She had built a life for us that was simple and functional, and I rarely felt that anything was missing. We had two rooms and a kitchen, the morning paper, and we often went to the Skansen open-air museum on the weekend. Sometimes her friend Lilian would come over for dinner, and they would sit at the kitchen table laughing and smoking long after I had gone to bed. Falling asleep to the sound of their voices made me feel especially safe and secure. Lilian worked at the library, and she would bring me books that were no longer in circulation. They were battered and dog-eared, but it didn't matter. First it was tales about animals with sentimental illustrations, then adventure stories, mysteries and horror, Jules Verne and Edgar Allan Poe.

Mom was no reader, and I thought the library was a place for different kinds of people until I started going there in my early teens and had to drag myself away to go back home. I have often wondered what she thought of me as I sat there with my nose in a book, an occupation that must have seemed fruitless to her. But after she had come out with her usual suggestions that I should seize the day or go outside for some fresh air, she always accepted my choice with an indulgent smile.

In many ways I preferred being a child to being an adult. I wish I had more concrete memories from my childhood, actual evidence to return to. We didn't own a camera, so apart from a few photographs taken by Lilian's husband, Gösta, there are hardly any pictures of me. I was reserved but not shy, I probably didn't stand out in any particular way as far as my classmates were concerned, and I rarely reflected on how I came across to others. I was blessed by the self-sufficiency of childhood, and I sometimes think it has never really left me.

One summer we borrowed a cottage in the archipelago from one of Mom's work colleagues. I don't know how it came about, but maybe someone took pity on the young single office clerk with a son and allowed us to use the place for a few weeks.

It was a fantastic summer, possibly still the best in my whole life. I felt like a character in the adventure stories I loved as I leaped and ran over the sun-warmed rocks, with the smooth flat stones and rough lichen beneath the soles of my feet. My skin was tanned by the sun, I swam, I dived, I fished. It was almost a primitive existence, archaic even, although of course I didn't have the words to describe it that way back then. In the evenings we stayed up late and watched the sun go down, saw the tops of the mountain pines silhouetted against the orange sky. It felt as if something reached inside my chest and squeezed my heart, gave me a thrilling realization that the world was truly wonderful, and that I needed nothing else at that moment. Right there and then, life seemed perfect.

I remember thinking: This is how I want to feel in the world.

Because I was a bookworm, I was transferred to the school in Södermalm. I realized that the quality of education there was better, but I wasn't happy. The teachers were old and strict, and I felt as if I had simply played through life until now, when I had to compete for my grades with classmates who were completely different from those in Älvsjö. Their families and their ways and habits were not the same, they were self-confident and seemed worldly-wise even though they were in their early teens. And yet we were only in the Söder district of the city, which at that time was largely poor and run-down. I used to imagine with horror what it would have been like if I'd been sent to the school in Östermalm.

For the first time I noticed that those around me re-acted to the fact that I didn't have a father. In Älvsjö no one had cared, although the people there were probably less well-educated and enlightened. And yet they were more tolerant. In addition, I hadn't been the only one in that situation at my previous school, whereas in Södermalm I was regarded as different. Exotic, perhaps, or maybe just poor and weird.

Many of my classmates seemed to be carrying the weight of history, something that anchored them in the world, while I felt as if I were bobbing around on the sur-face. It's possible that they themselves thought of that his-tory as both good and bad, but I saw only the good points: stability, summer cottages, money, ancestors. They came from families that had achieved things for generations, their fathers had titles, they went away on vacation. One of them even had a housekeeper.

In comparison to them my existence appeared paltry, my whole life seemed small. It consisted of Mom and me, and we rarely did anything special. We didn't really have anyone to visit, we never traveled, and I never had any exciting stories to tell.

I remember my childhood and youth as a series of fragmentary images, all striving in the same direction. They were about conquering the world, making it my home—pretty clumsily, at first. One summer day I attempted to build a tent in the garden, because I'd read an adventure story where the main character camped out in the countryside. There were vivid descriptions of the stars twinkling in the dark sky, and all the sounds of the night came alive for me: an owl, a dog, plus something unidentifiable, a large animal some distance away.

I wanted to experience the same excitement, the same feeling of being at the mercy of nature, but nature in our garden wasn't much more than a sparse patch of grass, a few pine trees, and some spindly bushes. Mom suggested that I could spend a night on the balcony instead. If we draped a blanket over two chairs, it would almost be like a tent. It was actually a good idea, less complicated and less scary, but it was the scary part I longed for. I wanted to take a risk.

Needless to say there was no money for a tent, and we didn't know anyone who owned one. I struggled for hours trying to build one: I hunted out suitable branches in the forest, slender and strong, and then I did my best to link them together by pushing their clefts into one another to form something that I imagined resembled the framework of a Native American tent. Time and time again it fell apart, and in the end I was on the point of giving up.

Then Sören appeared in the doorway of the neighboring property. He was a student in his early twenties, and he would often stop and chat with me. He was usually on his way somewhere: to the Royal Institute of Technology, where he was studying civil engineering, or to meet friends and girls. He came home late at night, wobbling along on his bicycle, and he would play music with the window wide open. To me, his life was the essence of freedom. He came from Örebro and his apartment was a sublet. He looked after himself and did whatever he liked. Sometimes he would sit in the garden wearing small sunglasses and reading a thick book about thermodynamics or the mechanics of materials, smoking a cigarette. If the books hadn't seemed so boring, I would happily have swapped places with him.

"Hi, how's it going?" he called out when he spotted me and my collapsed tent.

I had to admit that it wasn't going too well. Sören nodded understandingly, then he pointed to the rug beating frame a short distance away.

"There's your tent framework," he said.

The fact that I hadn't thought of it myself was embarrassing, because all I had to do was drape the blankets over the lower part, and there was my tent. I ran upstairs to our apartment and fetched one of the plastic mats from the balcony, which meant I could sit comfortably on the floor of the tent. Sören joined me and lit a cigarette.

"Not bad," he said.

After a little while he had to hurry off to his summer job at the Konsum grocery store in Västberga. I lay down and read by flashlight in my tent, but by ten o'clock I had to give up. The ground was cold and damp and a great big earwig suddenly crawled across the page. I went back up to the apartment.

A few years later I had stopped playing games and Sören had completed his education. He immediately got a job with the Gas and Water Company in the city and left home dead on time each morning, wearing a suit and tie. Occasionally he invited me up to his little two-room apartment. He would put a Benny Goodman album on the record player and mix us both a grog. We would sit beside each other on his balcony in the evening sun, slowly sipping our drinks. I didn't really like the taste, even though my grog never contained more than a splash of alcohol. However, it made me feel grown-up, and before long there was a pleasant fuzziness in my head, a softness, as if I had become at one with the world in a new way.

Sören had started dating a girl called Lillemor, but he rarely mentioned her to me, which I was pleased about. My lack of interest in that part of his life was compounded by a stab of childish jealousy over the fact that she also sat on his balcony with a glass of grog sometimes. I preferred other topics, such as Sören's stories about fishing, which he had enjoyed in the summer when he was growing up, and still did from time to time. He was interested in music, but not in literature; in nature, but in a concrete and practical way. I might not have been able to put it into words back then, but I understood that Sören wasn't a romantic like me. Deep down he seemed contented with his life. He was a nice person, which made an impression on me. His stories might not have been particularly exciting, but they were characterized by a kind of quiet conviction. He didn't go fishing because he had a passion for fishing, he went fishing because his father used to go fishing—you just went fishing, and that was that.

One summer he took me with him. We got up early in the morning and caught the ferry to Vaxholm, and from there we sailed out to an island on a smaller boat. Sören had prepared the excursion with care, he was carrying fishing tackle, including two rods, plenty of food, and a seat pad rolled up beneath his full backpack. It was a peaceful day, there was a silvery haze in the air that gave the archipelago a pale gray shimmering quality. The sky, the sea, and the rocks flowed into one another, it was as if we were enclosed in a soft, gentle mist. He had brought coffee, orange juice, fried-egg sandwiches, and a packet of cookies that hadn't traveled too well. As we sat side by side on a flat rock and tucked into our picnic, I thought it was the most delicious food I'd ever eaten.

He showed me how to cast, and I learned quickly. Then my reel kept sticking and Sören began to investigate what the problem was. In the meantime I went for a walk around the island. There was a little shore on the far side. I jumped from rock to rock along the water's edge, some of them were covered in seaweed that had dried out in the warm sunshine. Reeds and rubbish had been washed up among them, a piece of rope, a broken glass bottle. Beaches prompt the imagination, they provide an opening onto the sea and the world, a promise of something bigger. Like a child I hoped to find treasure or a message in a bottle, something valuable or thrilling that had been in the sea for many years, only to be discovered by me. All I found was a battered float, but even that made me happy, and I put it in my pocket.

When I got back Sören had fixed my rod, and with the first cast I caught a pike. It was fascinating, literally feeling nature grab ahold of the other end of the line. The whole rod jerked, and I shouted to Sören to tell him I'd gotten a bite.

"Just take it easy," he said, but I felt a surge of panic at the thought of bringing in the fish. The weight and resistance in the rod made me think it would reach a breaking point and snap in half. I would never have believed that a fish could thrash around so much. Above the surface of the water it was like one huge shimmering green muscle, floundering and twitching in spasms on the hook. Sören broke its neck with a practiced hand and laughed sympathetically at my ashen face. I thought fishing was an enjoyable pastime as long as you didn't catch any fish.

The story of my pike lived on over a weak grog on Sören's balcony. He exaggerated my fear, but also the size of the fish, until in the end it sounded as if I had achieved a heroic feat.

"Have you been with Sören?" Mom would sometimes ask when she could smell the smoke on my clothes, and maybe the faint whiff of alcohol on my breath. I was actually too young to drink, but she took a pragmatic approach: It was never more than one glass, so it wasn't worth mentioning.

Our friendship gradually fizzled out. Sören fell in love with someone other than Lillemor and moved to Hammarbyhöjden with his new girlfriend. Our goodbye was unsentimental.

"Give me a call sometime and we'll have a grog," Sören said, but I never got around to calling him and he didn't call me either.

Another image: I read Hjalmar Söderberg's *Doctor Glas* several times, not least because I thought the restaurant visits were so appealing. The doctor in the novel went to Strömparterren, Djurgårdsbrunn, and Hasselbacken, names that breathed a kind of old-fashioned bourgeoisie that both attracted and scared me. I pictured upholstered furniture and velvet, cigars and punch. Some of the things they ate and drank were a mystery to me—potage à la chasseur or Manzanilla—but other things sounded delicious and incredibly elegant: a couple of sardines and a few brined olives as a snack, simple but Continental, fillet of sole, quail, fruit, always Chablis with the meal. I had never tasted Chablis, but I knew it was a white wine, and I could see the glass right there in front of me, misted with condensation in the late-summer warmth.

Going out and eating a meal like that was of course an impossibility, as unattainable as traveling to the moon. It was hard to understand how much people paid for food in a restaurant compared with what it cost to eat at home. However, the thought of it was so tempting.

"I suppose it's nice to avoid the washing up," Mom once said laconically when I brought up the subject.

Work was important when I was growing up. A permanent post was the best thing you could possibly have, even though it wasn't too difficult to secure one back then. My mother was always nagging me to get a job during the school holidays. She didn't like inactivity, and I realized that although she never came right out and said so, she perceived my reading as exactly that. A part of me would have loved to stay in bed all morning with a book, but I got myself jobs and worked conscientiously.

After a few years of working in warehouses it occurred to me that I ought to be able to find employment where I could read at the same time, and once I'd managed to do that and gotten used to it, I wondered why everyone didn't do this. I felt as if I had outwitted the system as I sat on a folding chair outside the toolshed at the cemetery in Västberga, where I had plenty of time to look after the graves and the lawns, and could let my breaks run on.

Because I still lived at home, I didn't have much expenditure. I started paying Mom a token sum for food and rent during the months when I was working, but otherwise my money was mine to spend as I wished. One day

I realized that I could actually afford to go to a restaurant. This led to a great deal of pleasant musing: Which restaurant should I choose? Obviously Mom would be my dining companion, but of course she protested.

"It's not necessary," she said as she so often did. "I'm not going to eat up your money."

But going alone was unthinkable, and none of my friends would have understood the point of the exercise.

I decided on the Opera Bar. I thought the decor there would be something special, maybe the closest you could get to a Söderberg novel. Mom and I sat side by side on the overheated bus into town, uncomfortably dressed in our best clothes. We arrived looking kind of crumpled, our foreheads shiny with sweat, as nervous as if we were about to commit a crime.

We went inside and were confronted by a maître d' standing behind a lectern. He asked tersely if we had a reservation.

We didn't, of course. Neither of us had thought it would be necessary.

The place really was astonishing, a fantasy world. I had never seen anything like it. We stood there in silence, admiring the beautiful ceiling with the rosette-shaped windows. It reminded me of a cathedral. The shelves behind the bar were made of dark wood, and bottles in every color of the rainbow shimmered in the light, full of promise.

When the maître d' saw our disappointed faces, he softened.

"Try Bakfickan," he suggested. "There's bound to be room in there."

Bakfickan turned out to be right next door to the main restaurant, and there was indeed room for us. I could see straightaway that it wasn't as elegant, but it had something else. It felt modern, it was less formal, you didn't need to be dressed up—almost the reverse. The walls were covered in ceramic tiles with abstract blue designs, rhythmic and playful, like jazz. *Sören would like this place*, I thought.

It was a fantastic evening. The menus were beautiful, but the food sounded uncomplicated. To begin with Mom didn't seem too impressed; it was the kind of food she thought she could have prepared at home. But I also noticed that she appreciated the details—the smooth linen napkins, the bread basket, the little dishes of butter. The lighting was pleasant, there was a gentle hum of conversation, and when the waiter asked what we would like to drink, I ordered a bottle of Chablis.

To be honest, a whole bottle of wine was too expensive, but asking for a glass each would have felt like a cheap gesture on an evening like this, and two glasses each cost almost the same as a bottle. It was also well worth the expense to have the waiter bring the bottle over and open it at the table. He sniffed the cork, then poured a small amount into my glass and waited for me to taste it.

Needless to say, it was the most delicious wine I had ever drunk. I could see that Mom liked it too, even though she never drank wine. She was enjoying the whole thing: the little charade with the tasting, the silver bucket filled with ice in which the bottle sat while we ate and drank. We were suddenly talking to each other in a new way, as if we were two equal adults sitting there. I watched as she became more and more relaxed. At first her entire being had radiated the conviction that this kind of restaurant wasn't for the likes of us, but gradually her body language softened with the help of the wine, her cheeks grew pink. I thought I would do anything to be a person for whom being in an environment like this was perfectly normal.

I was excited for several days afterward. I felt as if I had pushed open the door to a different kind of life, a life that played out in the city, among bars and restaurants, theaters and cinemas, among people who were also inter-ested in living that sort of life. I also realized that money was essential, I wanted to eat more meals in restaurants, and I wanted to travel in cabs. There were shops with tantalizing displays of clothes and shoes, records and books. I wanted to be able to go in and buy something, something new, something that would turn me into a per-son with both fashionable shoes and knowledge about the latest music and literature. I felt as if I had never experienced the city for real, never understood what a city had to offer.

Mom gave a skeptical smile when I tried to explain it to her.

"So the library isn't good enough for you anymore?" she said when I talked about the big bookstore on Humlegårdsgatan. She made me feel a little embarrassed, but at the same time I knew that she was content with her life in a way that I would never be.

I couldn't stop thinking about taking Sören to Bakfickan, so one afternoon I looked up his name in the phone book then set off on my bicycle to Läckövägen in Hammarbyhöjden, where he lived. It was a warm, lazy, early-summer afternoon, the sun was blazing down and there was no wind. The ride was so easy that with hindsight it seemed kind of creepy, like an omen.

I had no problem finding the address. The stairwell was cool, and according to the list of names inside, Sören and Lisen lived on the second floor. I went upstairs and pressed the bell firmly.

It was a while before anyone came. I heard muted sounds from inside, followed by slow footsteps, then the door was opened by a woman who was beautiful but looked tired, as if the bell had woken her.

"Yes?" she said.

"I'm looking for Sören. My name is Gunnar Abrahamsson. We used to be neighbors, in Älvsjö."

She nodded. "Yes, he talked about you. You'd better come in."

I followed her through the narrow hallway and into the living room. The Venetian blinds were partly closed, and the bright sunshine outside made stripes on the wallpaper.

She nodded toward a low teak sofa upholstered in a bobbly green fabric that looked like moss, and I sat down.

"Maybe you're too young to drink?" Lisen was standing in front of a liquor cabinet mixing herself something in a heavy crystal glass.

"No, I'd like one please," I said.

She placed my glass on the coffee table and sat down beside me. She took a sip of her drink, then inhaled deeply.

"Sören is dead."

It was a bizarre sentence, one of the worst I'd ever heard. It was also the first time I'd heard those words about a person who had meant something to me. Until that point I had been spared any contact with death, all my elderly relatives were still alive, and to be honest I saw them so rarely that their deaths wouldn't affect me greatly. I had only read about funerals in books. To me death was an aspect of fiction or nature: a dead bumblebee, a dead flower. Dead was an adjective among many others.

"What do you mean?"

She repeated the short sentence, which sounded even worse this time.

"How?" I said eventually.

"It happened just over a month ago. They found him in the water off Långholmen."

"Was he fishing?" I asked, and immediately saw from her expression that it was a childish question.

"They think...he might have done it himself."

"What? You mean...he took his own life?"

119

She nodded.

"I don't know how well you knew each other," she said quietly, "but he was good at hiding it. He suffered from periods of depression. Sometimes he would disappear, he could be gone for weeks without getting in touch."

It was unbelievable. How could people have such secrets? Once again I felt childish for not having realized, not having had the faintest idea that all wasn't well with Sören.

The grog was much stronger than the ones he used to mix, it had a bitter taste. There were tears in Lisen's eyes now. Personally I have never found it easy to cry, even though I am essentially a sentimental person.

She reached for a packet of cigarettes on the table and lit up.

"He was buried last week. In Örebro, where his family lives. It was a weird occasion. I'd only met them once before in passing, and now we were together under these awful circumstances. And no one wanted to talk about what had happened. I think they found it shameful."

Her skirt had ridden up her thighs, exposing pale, smooth skin. I found it hard to tear my gaze away. She noticed that I was looking at her, and her expression was intense as she stubbed out her cigarette in the ashtray on the table. She gave an impression of experience, as if she were older than her years. As if she had already seen most things. The atmosphere in the room had changed, the silence between us was dense and highly charged. It was the first time I had encountered that kind of silence, the silence that comes just before something happens.

A flash of insight into human nature came to me, an insight into how tempting something forbidden can be, precisely because it is forbidden. This was serious, I thought, this was real life. Her perfume was sharp, a scent I wouldn't usually have liked, but right now it was hugely arousing. Her skin glowed beneath her makeup as she leaned forward with that same intense look in her eyes and kissed me. Her kiss was also intense, as if something special were at stake. She took my hand and placed it on her thigh.

I realized that we were in a state of emergency, so to speak. She wouldn't normally have paid any attention to someone like me, but right now we were welded together by our sorrow, like two shipwrecked souls who had no one but each other.

The apartment was stuffy and unaired. Beneath the cigarette smoke lay the dry smell of warm wood from the parquet flooring, dust motes danced in the air in front of the venetian blinds. Everyday life was continuing outside. Housewives were heading home with bags of groceries so they could make a start on dinner, husbands were returning from the office, children were playing among the pine trees.

Lisen's whimpering made me understand that what was going on between us was on a different level from the rest of that everyday life—a primitive, primordial level. She sounded like a young animal, a creature I had to take care of. Suddenly I was in charge, our roles had switched as soon as she placed my hand on her thigh. The situation was new to me, and yet I intuitively knew what to do—not because of the scraps of information that I had snapped up from a classmate's well-thumbed magazines but because of a latent knowledge that surprised me. I'm sure I came across as fumbling and inexperienced, but she was very sweet to me afterward. She rested her head on my chest, and although we didn't talk about what we had just done, I felt close to her.

When I got home that evening with the sharp scent of her perfume still clinging to my shirt, I was a different person. Life had given me a crash course in being an adult and I had passed with flying colors, I had been confronted by life and death in the same afternoon.

I think it somehow showed. I didn't mention what had happened to anyone, but I could feel it in my posture: I exuded a quiet dignity, an awareness of life's mysteries. It made me behave like an interesting person.

Eva and I were in the same class, and in our last semester at high school we became a couple. It was undramatic, maybe even unromantic. She had decided that she wanted me, and I didn't have particularly strong views on the subject, so I thought I might as well give it a go. Neither of us had been in a previous relationship, and after the fumbling frisson of the initial period, we quickly became like an old married couple.

Mom and Eva would sit in the kitchen in the evenings chatting and laughing like two friends of the same age.

I reluctantly came to the conclusion that they were very similar. Eva was from a simple family, and seeing her and Mom side by side suddenly filled me with revulsion. There was something ordinary, something unsophisticated about the two of them, and although I loved and respected my mom, it seemed to me that they brought out the worst in each other. They gabbled away and laughed at things I just didn't find funny. That was the problem with Eva: I thought the stuff she laughed at was too simple; she was cheerful and pretty but our conversations were never about anything in particular.

It was as if the experience with Lisen had ruined me, or at least given me a taste for something that was out of reach. I might not have wanted Lisen, but I wanted to repeat the feeling of having the unattainable. I wanted something other than what was available to me, which was a troubling realization. And I also knew, even though I couldn't put it into words, that Eva would hold me back.

I did my military service as a signalman in Skövde—a wasted year, I thought at the time. The Västgöta plain was gray and windblown, and I constantly longed to be somewhere else. Not necessarily at home, but somewhere else. I wanted to read and work: to read about love and death, about subjects that meant something, to work to set myself free. When I was finally allowed to return home, that was exactly what I did. I never had a plan, a greater purpose in anything I chose to do, and looking back I think it's remarkable that I got as far as I did, given that there are plenty of people with much bigger dreams who never even got halfway.

"The world is fire; become fire, and you will have a place in the world," it said in a book I read. I thought that was a perfect line, youthfully passionate and romantic. At the same time I knew that I wasn't the kind of person who would burn, at least not as strongly as certain others. I preferred to keep my distance and observe their fires, edge closer occasionally in order to warm my hands.

I met Marianne in the autumn of 1969. She was studying law and was politically active, mainly to annoy her parents I think. She had grown up in Gnesta, a community built around the railway, and I fell in love with her when she told me how as a child she had loved to stand at the station, watching the trains and the signs showing their destinations, dreaming of places that might not have been exotic but were at least different.

Her elderly father had been a manufacturer, a profession that sounded old-fashioned even then, like something out of a 1930s comedy. She had grown up with good manners and had an air of sophistication, a way of assuming that there would always be someone there to light her cigarette. Which there always was, of course, and I was one of them. Maybe she chose me to annoy her parents as well. She had blond hair that she bleached to make it even lighter, she seemed so worldly-wise, and she spoke fluent French in a deep, slightly hoarse voice. In many ways she reminded me of Lisen, especially the feeling that I had acquired something that was actually out of my reach. It was as if the universe had taken pity on me and let my wish come true, like in a fairy tale.

I thought that Marianne had understood the essence of life, and that she would therefore understand me. Perhaps that was the real reason why I wanted her: not so much for her own sake as for mine. I also liked the thought of how we looked together, we made an attractive couple. I have always tried to stage my life, to a certain extent. It might be superficial, but it is innocent. It is a way of continuing to play.

Marianne liked to talk about politics, a topic that has never really interested me, and in her company it made me very uncomfortable. She was a dyed-in-the-wool Social Democrat, which appeared to be an act of rebellion against her maternal grandparents, who were committed to the Center Party. And yet I was the one who felt tongue-tied and bourgeois when Marianne and her friends were discussing social issues. They were dedicated leftists, directly opposed to their parents' convictions. She often wanted to tell me about "the people," an expression I myself would never use, even though I knew a lot more about the section of the population she was referring to than she ever would. Sometimes we argued, much to her delight, only to reconcile quickly in bed. She regarded me as a cultivated barbarian, a wild creature that she had tamed, making it possible to bring me into the elegant salons where she and her friends sat around despising the bourgeoisie.

"Gunnar writes wonderful poetry!" she would exclaim, and everyone's eyes would turn to me with polite curiosity.

I didn't. I wrote poetry, but it wasn't particularly good. It mimicked the poetry that had meant something to me, old-fashioned poetry that I had absolutely no desire or intention of sharing in front of her friends, who already regarded both me and my suit with skepticism.

It was obvious that Marianne and I were an ill-matched pair. Mom said exactly that on one occasion, and she never needed to mention the matter again, because we both understood what she meant.

It was Marianne who said I ought to study. The idea had crossed my mind in the past, but I hadn't really known how to go about it. Sören was the only person I knew who'd been to a university. I also thought students were very different from me: single-minded, politically engaged. They protested on the streets, occupied their own student union building. Some of Marianne's friends had been involved, and she would talk excitedly about what they had done, while to me it seemed like totally stupid behavior. We argued about it more than once.

"You must have gotten good grades?" she said. I had, more because I found it easy to learn than because of discipline and hard work, but the evidence was there in black and white. Marianne helped me to fill in the application, and when the news came—I had been accepted in the philosophy course at Stockholm University—she stole a bottle of champagne from her father and we toasted my success in paper cups on a bench on Fjällgatan.

I hadn't a clue what I was going to use my studies for. As far as Marianne was concerned, higher education was a given, and maybe she persuaded me to go for it largely for her sake. She didn't want to be with someone who spent his days doing the same kind of low-paid work as the people to whom she was theoretically so committed. She thought being a student was wonderful, everyone she hung out with was a student. Presumably that was also what her parents expected of her boyfriend.

I tried to explain to Mom, who was very pleased that I had gained a university place but found it difficult to understand why I hadn't chosen some kind of proper training.

"You're so calm and patient, you'd make a good dentist," she said. Instead I would be sitting at home reading books, as usual.

"I thought you'd already read them all," she joked, then she became serious, wanting reassurance that I wasn't planning to resign from my job.

I wasn't. I worked and studied at the same time, putting in late nights as a station attendant on the subway. During the week I was often able to get quite a lot of reading done, because there were so few passengers.

At the end of my first year at the university I applied for and got a job delivering the internal mail at Rydéns publishing house. The idea of literally being surrounded by literature appealed to me, but once I'd started I quickly realized that the work had very little to do with the actual books. Even so, I was happy. It was a fascinating environment, the building was right in the middle of the city and was no more than ten years old, designed especially for the publisher by one of the leading architects of the day. It had an air of exclusivity: The foyer gave the impression of a hotel lobby, as if you had traveled to a foreign country with the help of literature. There were comfortable armchairs between the built-in bookshelves, which made a small library comprising books published by Rydéns. On the wall by the elevators was a shimmering mosaic: a simplified version of the muse of poetry lifting her writing tablet to the sky—and to the upper floors, where literature was created.

Even the basement had been thoughtfully designed and decorated, although it wasn't as elegant as the rest of the building. The department where I checked in, along with the janitors and receptionists, had a very nice coffee room, and the mail room was practical and pleasant, despite the lack of daylight. A radio played all day, and everyone was friendly toward me.

Sometimes Marianne complained that we didn't see each other very often, and that I arrived late to parties and left too early. But on the whole I think she was happy with our relationship, which gave us both a great deal of freedom.

However, just before the start of the autumn semester she informed me that she was leaving me, because she had fallen in love with a young lawyer at the practice where she had worked as a clerical assistant over the summer.

I think I was more hurt by the rejection than upset at losing her. And I was angry. Of course someone like her wouldn't really want someone like me. Of course she wanted a lawyer, someone with a future that promised status and financial stability. Suddenly, being a student seemed childish, not to mention being a mail boy. Marianne had gotten herself a summer job that was a step toward her career in law, while I made do with a job that absolutely anyone could have done.

I drank myself into a stupor for several nights in a row, showed up at work on time but tired and scruffy.

Lars Löf was the head of publishing back then. He was a genial man in his fifties, chubby and boyish. "Morning, morning!" he would call out to everyone he saw when he arrived, including me. Occasionally I would risk lingering by the bookshelves in the foyer for a few minutes, leafing through some recent publication. Rydéns published a series of classics, some translated for the first time and some in new translations, with forewords by celebrated authors. It was a beautiful series, small and bound, with a design that was modern and classic at the same time. Ovid's *Metamorphoses* was the latest, it had an intense green cover, glowing like a row of emeralds on the shelf.

"Morning, morning!" Lars Löf's voice was right behind me. I jumped, feeling somehow caught out.

"Good morning," I said.

He smiled at me.

"These are lovely," I said, mainly for the sake of saying something, and held up the Ovid.

"There's nothing wrong with the content either," he replied cheerfully.

I'm sure he didn't mean to be patronizing, he wasn't that kind of person, but I suddenly felt under pressure. My head was aching.

"No, I know," I said in a tone of voice that might have been a little sharper than the situation warranted.

He raised his eyebrows. "Have you read it?"

"I read it when I was little."

That wasn't entirely true, I had read an illustrated children's version, a dog-eared reject from the library that Lilian had brought home for me, but as far as I could tell all the key elements had been there.

"You know something?" Lars said. "I don't think everyone who worked on it has necessarily read it." He laughed, a clucking little laugh. "Take it if you'd like to read it again," he said, nodding at the book. "The translation came out really well."

He turned to the receptionist.

"Morning, morning!" he said to her before setting off toward the elevators.

The whole thing seemed deeply symbolic, I thought as I sat in my bed in the evenings reading Ovid, slowly realizing that I too had to become someone else. Since no god or benefactor was going to materialize and help me out, it was up to me to make it happen. All my life Mom had said, "If you want something done you have to do it yourself." She had never relied on someone else.

There are times in our lives when it really feels as if we are holding our destiny in our hands, and we can decide which direction it will take. I couldn't do anything about the fact that Marianne had left me, but I had no intention of letting something like that happen again— not because I had nothing to offer, or because I appeared uninteresting in comparison to someone else. And if I really did want the life I'd read about in so many books, then I couldn't continue being a station attendant and mail boy. That was a dead end, a comfortable one admittedly, but it would never lead to insights about what life really had to offer. I didn't want to be a person who lives his entire life constantly feeling that something is missing, that things should be different. I had just been reading Rilke, and his words echoed in my head: "You must change your life." I felt as if he were addressing me directly, and I had to obey.

The following morning I was waiting for Lars Löf by the bookshelves in the foyer.

"Morning, morning!" he said cheerily when he saw me. "So what did you think of the Ovid?"

"The translation really is excellent," I said. "It's an important publication."

"Oh?" he replied with a little smile.

"There can't be many works that have had greater significance for both art and literature," I said. My voice wasn't completely steady. "Apart from the Bible, of course. Actually, I was wondering... whether there might be any jobs on one of the other floors?"

Lars Löf's expression was kindly, but he was clearly surprised.

"You mean in one of the editorial departments?"

"Yes." I cleared my throat. "I'm studying philosophy at the university at the moment, and I'd very much like to help out upstairs. Maybe in the nonfiction department, or preferably fiction if there's anything available. I have no training and I understand it might be difficult at this time of year, in August, but I thought maybe I could be useful later on, in the autumn." I paused to catch my breath. "Oh, and I read a lot. I've read most things."

"You're on the internal mail at the moment, aren't you?"

I nodded.

"In that case I'm sure we can make better use of you upstairs. Come and see me at lunchtime and we'll talk it over."

And so my career began. It was so astonishing that it took a long time before I realized that was what was happening. No one I knew had pursued a career, no adult I had ever known. You got a job, and you kept it. Permanent employment was the ultimate proof that you were a decent person, and once you were in that position it would be sheer hubris to want more.

Lars was both a kind and demanding boss. I started as an editor, working on some lightweight American novels that had been translated at speed and not especially well. The translators had no prestige, no artistic ambition; they worked quickly so that they would get paid quickly, and the worse the translation was, the greater freedom I had. I could make the text my own without anyone objecting, I could give it my rhythm, my nuances.

It was a strange, unspoken validation, knowing that the words in the finished book looked the way they did thanks to me. The fact that they weren't the kind of books I would have chosen to read didn't matter, I was proud and I was having fun. Every aspect of the work was effortless. I could see what was good in the original manuscript, what could be improved, and how to go about it.

When Lars realized that I had talent, he moved me over to translations of literary fiction, and after a few more seasons, to the place I had longed to be: the series of classics. My first task was to oversee a translation of Sappho's fragments—virtually the polar opposite of the work on the American novels I had started with. The translator was a pleasant but rigorous older lady, and there was no leeway within her words for my self-affirmation. Instead my role was to listen and be responsive, to bow to her knowledge without ignoring my feeling for the text. It seemed as if Sappho's words were winking through the millennia like shimmering pearls, and I wanted to give them the most beautiful setting possible.

Together with Lars I was allowed to draw up the list for the coming seasons in the classics series. It was intoxicating to be involved in choosing which of the greatest works of literature should be made accessible in Swedish, a dizzying feeling of contributing to something historic and magnificent. The other editors regarded what I was doing as a pretty dull job. They wanted to devote themselves to new literature, radical novels that would change the world, and they were happy to leave the classics to me.

The publishers were older and looked stern behind their spectacles and bundles of manuscripts, I found it easier to talk to Lars than to them. He was unexpectedly humble for a boss, and always listened to my suggestions. After a few years I had an idea.

"Couldn't we take the format of the classics series and use it to publish new literature?" I suggested during one of our very informal meetings at the coffee table in his office. "I don't mean exactly the same format, of course, but something cohesive that can become an imprint in its own right."

Lars raised his eyebrows. "And what would be the point of that?"

"To make it into a desirable entity—both for authors to be part of and for the readers who are going to buy them. If you like one book, you're going to want the rest. You're going to want them lined up on your bookshelf, you're going to talk to your friends about the latest in the series. For the authors, it will become a mark of quality to be published there. Once the series is established, all the young authors will come knocking on our door."

"All?" Lars said.

I realized I might have gone a little too far.

"All the ones we want to publish, anyway. Rydéns will have the most interesting debutants."

"It's not a bad idea," Lars said slowly. "But it has to be stylish, I don't want it to look as if we're starting a book club. Find someone who can give it youthful appeal."

"Me?"

"You can take care of this. Write down what you just said to me so that I've got something to show to the number crunchers. And jot down a few suggestions as to what we might publish. Come up with some ideas about the design. And a name. Find a good name."

It took a few years to establish Andromeda. I settled on the name when I was working on the Sappho book. "Andromeda has something better to offer." The line was as strikingly clear as an advertising slogan, a glowing, utopian promise of a better life, better literature.

I didn't have much of a network of contacts in the young literary world, so I had to try to build one up. At first I was understandably regarded with polite skepticism. I was the same age or even a few years younger than some of the aspiring authors I approached, but I came across as if I belonged to an older generation, with my love of the classics and my knowledge of the industry, passed down from Lars Löf. However, I could tempt them with Rydéns, with the status that being part of an old, world-class publishing house involved, while at the same time I was offering something new within its framework: a modern, attractive imprint. And then of course there were the legendary parties on the roof.

From a purely financial perspective it didn't go too well in the beginning, but Lars allowed me to continue. We grew close in a way that I think is typical for men of his generation: Our relationship was professional with occasional flashes of something personal, moments when he would confide in me. One afternoon he told me that he was in the middle of a divorce. His wife had met someone else and was moving out of their large apartment on Engelbrektsgatan. On another day he talked about his sister, who had been admitted to a psychiatric clinic. A cloud of sorrow passed fleetingly across his otherwise cheerful face.

"It's all so sad," he said before changing the subject.

I worked hard. The seasons followed one another almost seamlessly. There wasn't much else in my life back then, but I wasn't unhappy about that. Occasionally I would think about the painting of the staircase of age that used to hang in my maternal grandparents' farmhouse; I loved to gaze at it when I was little. As a child I had thought that the decades following childhood, on the way to the top, would be the best, a time of life when you were marching purposefully upward like an energetic mountaineer.

That was exactly what I was doing. I hardly noticed the passage of the years, but suddenly Mom turned fifty and I realized that she was getting old. Her hair was more gray than brown, and there was a weariness in her eyes and a slight stoop in her posture, both of which I associated with old people, those who had passed the top of the staircase and were on their way down the other side.

Her colleagues at work organized a small celebration with sandwiches and low-alcohol beer, and she came home carrying a large package that she proudly showed me: an engraved crystal bowl, sparkling like a huge gemstone, heavy and impressive.

That evening I took her to the Opera Bar, the Opera Bar itself, and this time I had reserved a table.

It is unfortunate that we are never fully aware when we are experiencing a golden age. Everyday life is everyday life, even during such a period. But when I think back to the eighties and the early nineties, I can see that it was a time with a new kind of energy. A time when literature felt glamorous, and the world surrounding it was desirable. I was standing right in the middle of it, and yet I was backstage. I promoted several authors who would end up in the history books. When an elderly critic with one of the broadsheet newspapers referred to "Andromeda literature," the publishing house congratulated me, rarely had a project turned out so well.

Many of my authors also became known outside the confines of the literary world. Some wrote books that were perceived as controversial, brave, they wrote about sex and violence, filthy but talented. Their pictures appeared in the press, they provided the perfect sound bites in interviews. Others tackled more conventional topics, but in a new way: Andromeda had found a perfect level between traditional and postmodern, between broad appeal and narrow focus. I had fun with my authors, and it was a fun time. I went to dinners and parties, I had love affairs. I was able to dabble in romance without too much thought, because I lived alone, free and unfettered.

And yet I couldn't shake off the feeling that it was largely pretense. That the generation of new, outstanding authors I had created weren't particularly outstanding after all—they were simply new. They would go down in history, no doubt about it, but would anyone be reading their books in a few years? In ten years, twenty, a hundred? Perhaps as interesting documents illustrating the period, but would anyone think they constituted good literature?

Sometimes I felt almost disgusted by the whole thing. I have never been drawn to what contemporary society values—quite the reverse. I have made it a point of honor to know that at least I am not an opportunist, that my driving force is what is best for literature not for my career. My sympathies have always been with those who have contemporary society against them. History's misunderstood souls. Those who have been written out of its annals in order to make room for names that have made sure they fit more easily into history's simplistic narrative about progress. Why didn't I publish something different, something that went against the accepted norm? These were bizarre thoughts in the context of an industry that existed to sell books, but if people wanted what I was giving them, then I instinctively sensed that something was wrong.

Rydéns took the opposite view, of course. I was regarded as a great asset and a promising prospect for the future. Lars Löf's crown prince.

I inherited that crown earlier than I had expected or hoped. One day he confided in one of those unexpected, intimate moments that he was suffering from an aggressive form of cancer, a few months later he was dead, and I was the editor in chief at one of the country's largest publishing houses. It sounded impressive, and Mom was proud—maybe that was the best thing about it, because added responsibility didn't make my job any more enjoyable, although I did appreciate the significant increase in my salary.

Suddenly I was a person with power. I admit that I was fascinated by certain aspects of my position, mainly by seeing the simple mechanisms of success reveal themselves so clearly. Colleagues who had previously treated me dismissively or churlishly started being nice to me, as if by magic. I could see straight through them, and it amused me to return their smiles while thinking that it was astonishing how predictable people could be, how transparent their behavior was. I also realized that success really does breed success. For some years my position made me interesting in other contexts too: If I had an opinion in a literary debate, the morning papers were happy to place their columns at my disposal, and since I was often the only one who held that particular view, I was given the opportunity to expand on it on TV sofas and radio programs. It was a brief taste of what it was like to be on the other side, to be in the limelight where so many of my authors had found themselves, while I remained in the background.

It soon became clear to me that I was in fact happiest in the background. Publicity gave me a creeping feeling that I was constantly on the verge of being exposed. Irrational, childish thoughts popped into my head, I was convinced that one day someone would realize that my lack of academic merit or killer marketing instincts made me unsuitable for the role of editor in chief, and would send me back down to the mail room.

I assumed that the board of directors at Rydéns were relieved when I kept a low profile. Sometimes I sensed that the views I had expressed in a newspaper article were at odds with what they had hoped I would say. However, they could see that I brought something else to the table that was valuable: an impression that Rydéns was a publishing house where a genuine intellectual exchange of ideas took place in an open-minded atmosphere, and where things happened. I never noticed it myself, but apparently it wasn't unusual for people to try to gate-crash our spring parties.

I often thought that my life would have been more cohesive if my father had shown up, but I stopped asking Mom about him when I was a teenager. "I don't know," she would reply whenever I brought up the subject, and in the end I decided to believe her. Even if she had given me an answer, it was hard to imagine what he and I would have said. The words we had wouldn't have been enough, we would have had to invent a new language.

I had Mom, I thought, it was just the two of us and that was fine.

And yet I fantasized well into my adult years about my father one day making an entrance into my life, and turning out to be both rich and famous. Or that he would at least make contact from beyond the grave, with a solemn lawyer as his earthly messenger, offering condolences on the death of my father and informing me that I had received a significant bequest. Or if not a bequest, then at least a story, a name, a place. I would have been proud if he had turned out to be a schoolteacher, that was a respectable profession, and his memory would have lived on in the minds of generations of students.

I had gotten to know many of my friends from my youth for the simple reason that we all liked reading books, but as the years passed our lives diverged more and more. They chose different careers, single-mindedly pursuing professorships and academic success, devoting their time and energy to activities that I perceived as more important and more worthy than selling books. Sometimes when we met up I felt superficial compared with them. Apart from two semesters studying philosophy, my only education was what I had learned during my years at Rydéns. I don't believe any of them thought there was anything wrong with my intellect, but I could feel myself shrinking in their company, next to them I saw myself as a salesman, first and foremost. At the same time, I knew that what most of them had in common was that they were following paths that in their eyes were self-evident, well-trodden by the generations that had gone before them, removing all obstacles in their way.

I often thought about the paths the generations before me had trodden: real paths along fields and across meadows. The stone walls you see everywhere in the Swedish landscape, the rocks carefully stacked on top of one another to divide the land—those walls were built by people like my relatives. They had dug stone after stone, rock after rock out of poor ground in order to make the land usable for farming, clearing anything that would impede the progress of the plow, piling layer upon layer with aching backs and calloused hands, simply to repeat the process the following day.

Today no one remembers the names of those who wore out their bodies in the fields, and in the churchyards their graves are long gone. But the stone walls remain, heavy with time, like silent monuments to forgotten generations of hardworking farmers.

Those stones were my history. There wasn't much I could lay claim to in this world, but those walls were mine. And I knew that no professor's son from Uppsala or the grandchildren of past generations' leading intellectuals would understand them the way I understood them, and that was exactly the way I wanted it to stay. As far as everything else is concerned I am a guest in your world, I thought, but the stones belong to me.

I had rarely seen Mom so upset as when Olof Palme was shot. She had a sticker with the red rose of the Social

Democrats on the kitchen bulletin board, but otherwise she didn't make too much fuss about her political convictions. She would never have joined a protest march, and she never talked about politics, although she did sometimes sigh when the TV news reported on a new round of cuts.

Three years later she was gone too, she simply dropped down dead, exactly the way she had said she hoped to go. One morning she collapsed in the laundry room, where a shocked neighbor found her shortly afterward.

I kept the red rose sticker when I cleared her apartment. In one of the cupboards above the closets in the hallway I found her fiftieth birthday present from the Customs Service, the large crystal bowl, still in its cardboard box. She had been so worried about it getting damaged that she had never used it.

I sat down on the floor and wept over that. And I wept over the drawings I found in a drawer, yellowing pieces of paper covered in a confusion of lines made with wax crayons, my exercise books and my reports from grade school. I wept over the passage of time.

It took several days to sort everything. I stood in the kitchen in the evenings and watched the sun set on everything that had been my life, on the only small history that I'd had. The last rays of the evening sun gave the pine trees in the yard glowing orange trunks, and I remembered the tops of the mountain pines silhouetted against the orange sky that summer when I was a child, when Mom and I borrowed the cottage in the archipelago.

And I thought that she was one of so many, of whole generations of Swedes who set off from the country to the city, who finally made it and built a new life there, slightly inept but well-meaning. Who with their hearts loved the old, but with their heads embraced the new: modern is good, light and hygienic is good, as are ideas that everyone thinks are good. Who sat there in the Swedish Housing Association's standard kitchen beneath the Swedish Housing Association's standard ceiling light, the white globe diffusing its milky glow. The stephanotis behind the TV was hung up with plastic hooks fixed with three steel pins, which were the only thing that could be forced into the solid wall. Beside it stood a linen press from a bygone era, polished wood with an inlaid pattern and a crocheted cloth, family photographs in dark frames. There were no photographs of grandchildren, something I was painfully aware of. The only child featured there was me, in pictures from a time as hopelessly lost as that of the linen press itself.

I called the Salvation Army. "Nobody wants furniture as big as that these days," said the woman. "We just can't sell it." I contacted a moving company who transported it to my office, and I left one of the photographs on display: me and Mom screwing up our eyes against the sun. I am wearing shorts and a striped T-shirt, she is in a blouse and skirt, bright yellow, although the picture is black and white. She has her arm around my waist and we are smiling: together, a unit, as self-sufficient as an island.

A few years after my mother's death, Susanne started at Rydéns. She worked in the sales and marketing department, and at first I didn't take much notice of her. She was one of many more or less identical young women who had passed through the same kind of post en route to the next step in their career, or maybe en route to an extended maternity leave that often began after they had gained permanent employment. They never stayed for long, and they weren't committed to the job on anything more than a superficial level. They showed up with big smiles and detailed documents about seasons and overambitious marketing schemes, good girls whose involvement was never wholehearted. I suppose there's nothing strange about it—that's how work functions. However, the fact that they could have been working on anything other than literature did bother me, in a way that I realized was irrational.

For the first time I didn't mind someone from sales and marketing sitting in on my meetings with authors. Susanne knew when to laugh and when to keep quiet, and she didn't have the forced enthusiasm that people who work in sales often have. She got to know the writers she would be working with, read their previous books or at least gave the impression of having done so. Our small talk by the coffee machine gradually developed into longer conversations that continued until the coffee had gone cold in our cups.

I hesitated for a long time before I decided to invite her to Bakfickan at the Opera Bar one evening after work, one of the evenings when we had both stayed later than everyone else and it was almost time for dinner. My life was uncomplicated, no one was waiting for me at home, no one would ask how I had spent the evening. I mentioned it in passing, keeping my tone casual: "I was thinking of going for a drink and something to eat, I don't suppose you'd like to come along?"

She seemed both surprised and pleased, she said she would love to come.

We're all allowed to make a few misjudgments in our lives. I only wish I hadn't done it with Susanne. Absolutely anything would have been preferable: a book that went badly, a huge marketing campaign that misfired. Money is only money when you have it.

The first evening flew by. We ate and drank and talked. She was funny, quick-witted, she made me laugh. Maybe I also laughed because I so wanted to laugh with someone. It had been a long time.

I was living in an apartment in Mariaberget then, and as I walked home across the bridge from Riddarholmen and Söder Mälarstrand it seemed to me that there was something magical about the evening, that the stars were twinkling at me and no one else. I was excited at having met someone who was so easy to talk to, someone I could have talked to for many more hours. It didn't happen often, and it felt special. I wanted to grab ahold of that feeling, make it stay with me. I wanted to see her again.

It was a few weeks before a good opportunity arose. As we sat there with our food and wine, I quickly realized that everything was different this time. I could tell that she wanted something from me, that she wanted this dinner with me to generate some kind of advantage for her. An advantage for her career, a favor to cash in. This became increasingly clear from the conversation, when she kept going back to the way in which whatever we were talking about would affect her. She also dropped hints that were anything but subtle. She was annoyed that she was one of the few members of staff who weren't allowed to go to the bookfair, she thought the authors she was working with weren't sufficiently well-known. There was even a problem with her office—it overlooked the rear courtyard. She mentioned it in passing, but she meant it.

I immediately saw her through fresh eyes: She came across as a calculating, self-obsessed child who wasn't really interested in spending time with me, and thought an evening in my company should be rewarded in some way, even though I was picking up the tab.

Nothing had actually happened, apart from two dinners, but everything immediately seemed dirty. I felt utterly stupid when I remembered walking home through the city a few weeks earlier in the early stages of infatuation, convinced that the stars were twinkling at me and no one else.

I find rejection difficult, that is something I have learned about myself. Suddenly I felt the same as when Marianne left me for the lawyer. It was a long time ago, but it didn't take much to open up the wound. Susanne's challenging smile across the table evoked the same rush in my brain, a rush that spread through my body as I realized that of course she hadn't gone home after our previous dinner with excitement bubbling in her breast but with the sense that she had played her cards right.

I am dispensable to everyone, I thought. *I am nothing. A fragment. Without a history, without anything to leave behind.* The rushing noise inside my head grew louder, became almost unbearable. It was as if a jet plane were taking off in there.

I don't remember what I said to her before I stood up and walked out. If I really tried I probably could remember, but I have done my best to forget. It was certainly worse than the situation warranted. I had drunk quite a bit, but that doesn't usually cause me to lose either my temper or my self-control. Maybe I had simply hoped for too much in a spirit of self-preservation, the years after my mother's death were the loneliest I had ever experienced. I was a solitary soul with no self-evident connection to anyone else, and at that time it didn't take much to give me hope.

Anyway, it was one of the most undignified moments in my life. Susanne owed me nothing, and I should have gritted my teeth and seen it for what it was—a dinner that had gone wrong—and never asked her out again. But it was as if all my emotions came together within that rushing sound, amplifying one another as if in a echo chamber, until I lost it.

The following day I was summoned by Rydéns's chief executive, Louise Enoksson, who had been appointed only a few months earlier. I had met her many times over the years and always found her very pleasant. Now, however, she was seated behind her desk with a grave expression on her face, and I felt like a schoolboy who had been sent for by the principal.

"Gunnar," she said in a sorrowful tone of voice, as if she were disappointed in me, which perhaps she was, "I hear you have behaved inappropriately toward a young female employee. Not only that, but she is someone over whom you have power in the workplace. She thought she was involved in a purely professional meeting, and found it extremely unpleasant when she realized that you seemed to expect something more."

"She was the one who expected something more," I said quietly, even though I knew the comment was unlikely to help my case.

"Apparently you also insisted on paying for these dinners," Louise went on. "She found that unpleasant too. She felt as if she had been bought."

The rushing sound filled my head again, and I had to bite my tongue to stop myself from yelling: "I'm just well brought up, for fuck's sake!" That's what I wanted to say, but instead I merely nodded.

Louise was Rydéns's first female CEO, and the whole situation was to her advantage. Going in hard on an incident like this made her look modern and justified her position. I could imagine people saying that a man would never have taken it seriously. At last things were beginning to move in the conservative world of publishing.

Technically I didn't lose anything that afternoon, but the uncertainty over who knew what about what had happened was terrible. It seemed to me that my colleagues couldn't look me in the eye when we met in the corridor. I would have liked to give them my version, admit that I had said something outrageous, but that the overall situation wasn't what they thought. However, it was impossible for me to do that. It would sound as if I were trying to lay at least some of the blame on Susanne, which was exactly what I would be doing. I knew how it would come across, it would only make my position worse.

I have never been interested in being liked by everyone, or even by the majority of people, but wondering who knew was troublesome. It infected my self-image in a way that I hadn't expected. What if the rumor spread outside Rydéns? What if I was the talk of the industry?

In the end I began to assume that was the case. I faced the world as if it were staring accusingly at me from all directions, I began to bad-mouth the world just as I presumed it was bad-mouthing me. It was like having contracted a chronic illness that I had to learn to live with: Life changed, and even though I tried to avoid thinking about it, I was constantly aware that it was slightly worse than before.

Almost twenty-five years had passed when Marianne and I met again. We were twice as old as we had been, yet I recognized her as soon as I saw her in a large group of people who were chatting and laughing. It was at the launch party for a new literary journal, nervous readings and warm white wine in a pretty inner courtyard on Nytorget, guests of all ages cheerfully mingling.

It was strange, seeing her again, like when the memory of a dream you had long ago suddenly flashes through your mind. I watched her from a distance for some time before going over to her. She had shorter hair than before but it was just as blond, she had fine lines around her eyes but was still strikingly beautiful.

She also had a divorce behind her and was the mother of three sons, I learned once we had put the initial awkwardness of meeting up again behind us and were standing at a wobbly bar table. The wall beside us was covered in honeysuckle in full bloom, and it enveloped our conversation in an almost unreal perfume.

"So what have you been up to lately?" she asked, smiling at me over her wineglass. Her smile was captivating, it lit up her whole face.

I didn't think I had much to tell. What had I actually done, apart from work? However, she seemed fascinated by everything I said. She kept on smiling when I told her where I was living. "It's only a two-room apartment," I explained, "but it's in an excellent location and the view is fantastic." She smiled when I told her I was an editor now, the editor in chief at Rydéns. It was clear that she found that sentence particularly attractive.

We went home together that night. We stood on my balcony and gazed out over the waters of Riddarfjärden, and she agreed that it really was a fantastic view. Then she kissed me. It felt both new and unfamiliar, an irresistible combination, and I could tell she felt the same.

Her father had died in the mid-1980s. Losing a parent is such a shattering experience that I imagined it would bind us together in a different way, but she seemed strangely unaffected by his death and showed no interest in talking about it.

I realized quickly and with disappointment that she had gone through life without anything making much of an impression on her, that she had remained a shallow person. There is no nicer way of putting it: Behind everything that was so fascinating before you really got to know her, behind her bubbling laugh and enchanting ability to tell stories, all the things that made her irresistible at a party or a dinner, made everyone who wasn't in her immediate company feel as if they had won the booby prize that night, behind the beautiful facade—and God knows it certainly was beautiful—there was nothing but emptiness.

Her personality was kind of mute, something within her was immobile. This wasn't the impression she gave in a fleeting encounter, quite the reverse, but I soon understood that in a way she was satisfied with life, or at least with herself, with the person she was. What mattered to her was what I regarded as the mere framework: home, career, vacations, diversions. I thought that the interesting part of life took place on a different level.

I know it was crazy for someone like me to embark on a relationship with someone like her. What was I hoping for? Maybe security, stability. It's not that easy to find a partner. Occasionally I thought I could have tried to meet a younger woman, but the experience with Susanne had left its mark, making the whole thing feel tainted, undignified. And I wasn't that kind of man, I told myself. I also thought it was romantic, the way Marianne and I had found our way back to each other after all those years. It was a good story, the kind of story people want to hear.

She often cheered me up. She had energy, she made things happen, and that appealed to me—I was the opposite. She threw parties, she always had a reason to add a little sparkle to our everyday lives, to do something spontaneous, to surprise me with an outing, to open a bottle of champagne on an ordinary Tuesday. I thought that life with her would be more colorful, more full of contrasts. She had a large circle of friends and acquaintances and seemed happy for us to do plenty of things separately, for me to stay home reading while she was out with a girlfriend. My somewhat introverted nature fit surprisingly well with her sociable inclinations. Plus it was hard to let go of the memory of the two of us when we were young, hard to forget how proud I had been because the most beautiful woman at the party wanted to talk to me, how proud I was that she still wanted to do that.

She had never completed her law degree. Instead she had gotten pregnant, then worked for a few years as an office administrator, then gotten pregnant again and again, and when she was coming to the end of her long-drawn-out maternity leave her father died, and there was no financial reason for her to work. She had inherited everything, the accumulated gains of a manufacturer's life, money from what I pictured as a *Fanny and Alexander* world, plus the lovely old manor house in Gnesta. She hadn't needed to work for many years, and she might never have done so again if she hadn't started to think that the role of a house-wife was kind of old-fashioned, when the children were older and better able to take care of themselves.

We moved in together and compromised on Vasastan. Marianne would have preferred to stay in Östermalm, but in Vasastan we could afford a six-room apartment. Even though I had always dreamed of having a big place in the city center, I thought the apartment was grotesquely large, a grandiose old residence with tiled stoves and bal-conies facing in two different directions. But the younger children needed their own rooms, and Marianne wanted a living room, a dining room, and a study. She also wanted to keep spending time in Provence, where she and her husband had owned a house. She had bought him out when she came into her inheritance. I didn't like the idea at all, particularly the thought of the house itself, the fact that someone else had lived there with her before me—someone she had left me for, back in the day. But she insisted that it was important to both her and the children, it was a part of their childhood. I had no way of counter-ing that argument.

It's so strange how life just happens. When I was young I thought that all important decisions were made after careful consideration, that detailed research lay behind every step that was taken, that every change followed a negotiation with oneself, that every aspect of life was the result of active choices. But actually, stuff just happens.

Marianne's eldest son was twenty-three and had left home long ago, the other two were fifteen and thirteen when we met, terrible ages I thought, even though I didn't actually know which age I would have preferred. My knowledge of children was very limited, I only really had the memory of my own childhood to turn to. Fredrik and Daniel fought and argued the whole time, when they weren't sitting passively in front of their video games. They would arrive at the dinner table with blank expressions and shovel down their spaghetti. I thought they were badly brought up, although Marianne seemed convinced that the opposite was true. They were rude and sulky, spoiled and self-obsessed. They had always gotten what they wanted and expected the world to go on treating them that way, as if they were on a vacation with never-ending free room and board.

I didn't see the point in following their development, because I didn't think either of them was developing in an interesting direction: They dabbled in sports, they had friends who were basically the same as them, they eventually chose educational courses that, in spite of their limited talents, would presumably one day secure them jobs that would make them rich. Still, I did make an effort, especially at the start. I took them to the movies and burger restaurants, I went to their soccer matches on the weekends, I gave them rides to visit their friends who lived out of town. However, I couldn't get past the feeling that we were completely different in every way, that all my efforts fell on stony ground. I had nothing to offer them that they wanted, which made me sad.

During the weeks they spent with Marianne and me, I constantly longed for them to go back to their father's place. I was suffused with a low-level sense of unhappiness in my own home, I was irritated by their socks and candy wrappers strewn everywhere, and thought Marianne should ask them to tidy up more often. They weren't particularly fond of me either, we accepted one another's presence because it was easier that way. Sometimes they asked me for money, and if I said no they sulked and there was a bad atmosphere, if I said yes I was disgusted with myself. I once suggested that Fredrik, who was the older of the two, should maybe get himself a part-time job—delivering leaflets or helping out in a store or café—but they both laughed at me as if it were a joke, and Marianne laughed too.

We married in a civil ceremony, quickly and with no guests, on a sunny but chilly day in late September. It was Marianne who wanted it that way, she'd already had a big church wedding, and said she was done with that kind of thing. I, who hadn't had the opportunity, thought that my only marriage ought to have taken place before God and a congregation, to the accompaniment of organ music. I would have liked to experience the occasion as something ceremonial, out of the ordinary. Instead it was a banal day, the registrar was almost robotically efficient, Marianne complained because the stiff breeze blowing off Riddarfjärden ruined her hair, we ate an early wedding dinner at the Grand Hotel, where I think we both realized we weren't quite as happy as the day demanded, that the conversation wasn't quite as relaxed and full of anticipation as at least I would have liked, so we both drank too much and fell asleep in no time in the expensive room we had booked.

And instead of building a family of my own, I took on hers.

I had never really made plans for children, a family. To be honest, I had never really made plans for anything. Maybe that was due to an inherited inability to dare to hope for too much from life. There is a difference between dreaming, which I have always done, and actually expecting life to develop in a certain way. Perhaps that was just how I was made: strong in my views about things that lay outside myself, weak in everything else.

I had somehow assumed that the question of a family would resolve itself, that sooner or later I would have one. I suspect it wasn't very important to me. I have never been fond of children, never longed for them or felt a biological urge to procreate. My hunger for life had always been about myself, first and foremost. I wondered if it was different if you were a more rounded individual from the start, or at least earlier in life. If you didn't have to get to know, examine, to a certain extent create both the world and your own character. If you were secure in the knowledge of who you were from the get-go, where you came from, where you were going. Or if you weren't going anywhere in particular, at least you were happy with that and didn't need to give the matter any more thought.

The realization that I would never have a family of my own brought no great or dramatic sorrow, but it did have an effect on me. It settled within me like a kind of low-frequency disappointment, a new base. I might not have been too interested in children, but I regretted that there was a part of life to which I would never gain access, that an experience which was clearly significant would be denied to me. Sometimes I thought a child would have been good for me, it would have made me ponder less and live more. Sometimes I thought I would have enjoyed teaching someone to fish.

After a while Marianne got a post with an interior design magazine. She was the kind of person who found work like that: not a dream job but a good job, creative, inoffensive, pretty well-paid. An occupation for the sort of person for whom work is mainly that—an occupation. The real money comes from somewhere else, the money that pays for your houses—it's not money you earn.

She got to travel a lot, attending conferences and design fairs, and she approached it all with enthusiasm. It seemed to me that this was because her character was so adaptable, she could have decided to throw herself into anything: charity, equine sports, children's culture. It just happened to be interior design. She founded a prize for young Swedish designers, initiated joint projects that resulted in highly desirable and expensive vases and bowls. "Swedish design has never been better!" she often said, and soon she had been saying it for a decade.

In the world where she worked, money and resources appeared to be inexhaustible, all ideas were received with enthusiasm, everything always seemed to be possible. I would never have said this to her, I would never even have hinted at it, but I quietly despised the whole thing. The poorly disguised advertorials and the badly rewritten press releases that she put her name on without a scrap of self-criticism, the ever-changing loyalty to the vagaries of fashion in order to avoid frightening off an advertiser: This spring, minimalism feels fresh and exciting, in the autumn we want baroque.

She swapped her former upper-class style of dressing for a new look: almost exclusively black clothes and striking accessories, dramatic shawls, big jewelry, always teamed with sneakers in gaudy colors. I hated them, but I could see that they made her appear youthful and relevant in the circles in which she moved. Her self-image was that she was a part of the cultural world, that she was doing something important.

I traveled a great deal between the ages of fifty and sixty, possibly as a manifestation of some kind of midlife crisis. A sense that my time was measured came over me: The proportion of the world I would manage to see during my life was limited, and dwindling with each passing day.

Marianne wasn't interested in going anywhere other than France. She didn't need any more of the world, whereas I really wanted to see every country in Europe. I wanted to tick off all the major or really old cities, the ones I had read about and imagined since I was young but had yet to visit. I hadn't traveled much earlier in my life, I had always thought it would be a bit sad to do it alone. I now felt that I had used my time wrongly, which was frustrating, and I needed to correct my mistake with some urgency.

I could justify many trips through my work. I was at a professional level where I was able to travel anywhere I wanted, as long as there was an acceptable reason. Apart from obvious destinations like the London or Frankfurt bookfairs, which could be complemented with a few days in Copenhagen or Berlin since I was out and about anyway, I would arrange meetings with an agent in Milan, an author in Paris. I visited other cities without an official mandate— a long weekend in Vienna, Venice, or Florence, traveling economy class but staying in a good hotel. My main aim was to see art and architecture, to wander the streets with no real plan in mind, to sit down at a sidewalk café and enjoy studying the menu and wine list, to order a glass of something and a snack, a bottle and a dinner on my own, listening to the languages being spoken all around me.

These trips were neither frivolous nor dissolute. Occasionally I might have company over dinner, someone I had fallen into conversation with. It was always a woman, a museum guide or a tourist staying in the same hotel, and now and again we might move on to another bar, but even though I can't deny that I was tempted, it never went any further. Sometimes I would tell them about Sweden, about the great authors and Nobel Prize winners I had met, but mostly I wanted to tell them about the art I had seen that day, how astonishing it was that it existed in reality, how miraculous it was to be alive and have the privilege of seeing it.

I liked the person I was to them. An educated Swede, pleasant and polite. A gentleman who paid the bill without expecting anything more, who said thank you and good night and nice to meet you. There was something beautiful about those fleeting encounters. After a while I began to think that maybe that was who I was, that my true self was fleeting, best suited to a few hours of socializing. That was when I came into my own, when I was still new in someone else's eyes and she was new in mine. When I was still a fragment around which you could weave a dream.

Maybe I was every bit as superficial as Marianne.

On the other hand, I felt completely the opposite inside the museums and galleries. That was where I really wanted to go, I spent hour after hour in the cool, quiet rooms, totally absorbed by the art on the walls. There was still so much in the world that I didn't know about, so much history to discover. The first time I saw Carlo Crivelli's paintings in the National Gallery I simply stood before them, overwhelmed. It was as if the Holy Spirit had sent his laser beam straight into my brain rather than Mary's as she knelt there on the canvas.

His work was technically perfect, the contours and colors unbelievably sharp. *How can this be from the fifteenth century?* I wondered. *How can it be so old and yet seem so untouched, so new?*

At the same time the pictures were idiosyncratic, for some reason small cucumbers had been painted at the edges. Something bizarre had crept into the elevated motifs of the Madonna and child, I didn't understand why, and it fascinated me. Crivelli could paint reality more vividly than reality itself, yet he included elements that made it both alien and more realistic. I saw the cucumbers as an image of the unexpected, something you couldn't have imagined. An illustration of the futility of believing that we can control our life, that it is supposed to form a narrative, to have an inherent logic. There was no logic in a few cucumbers on the edge of the Annunciation, which was exactly why I liked them.

What have I done with my life? I thought as I stood in front of the paintings. Many of my authors were regarded as great, but everything they had written was on a completely different level from the art around me. These paintings were a part of something eternal. To be surrounded by them was to make contact with something primordial. From a historical point of view, my authors were at best mediocre writers, neatly packaged by me and sold to a public that demanded nothing more.

Sappho writes: "Someone, I tell you, will remember us, even in another time." She was right, but she was also one of the few who would actually be remembered.

Almost everything disappears with the passage of time, sinking deeper and deeper into the layers of sediment that are the past. Even many of those who were highly thought of in their time finish up there, when the ideals prized in their time change. Paintings, books, people, most are forgotten. Nearly all of them.

Nothing I had helped to create would survive five hundred years into the future like Crivelli's paintings have. I would depart from this world without leaving any discernible traces behind, my name wasn't even included in the books that existed thanks to me. In just a few years there would be no one left who remembered me.

Then I was faced with a completely new situation: I developed heart problems.

Of course I did, I thought with a kind of resigned irony. My heart was the hardest-working organ in my body, it was my heart that had led me through my life. And now it had begun to beat irregularly.

"Did anyone in the family have similar problems?" the doctor asked. "This condition is often hereditary."

I was sitting on a bed in a cold examination room, with fluorescent lighting and a calendar adorned with a border of lingonberries pinned to the wall above the desk, where the doctor sat looking professionally sympathetic. Outside the window it was autumn, a clear and sunny autumn day. The trees glowed yellow, which seemed symbolic. Such beautiful weather, yet soon everything will die anyway.

"I don't know," I said, because I didn't know, and there was no longer anyone to ask. Mom had never mentioned a relative with a bad heart, but maybe that was what I had inherited from my father. Maybe he had died long ago from the same cause, maybe there was a long line of men with heart failure that was going to die out with me.

My body had never before limited what I could do. I had been spared most of the aches and pains that come with age, and I hadn't even noticed a drop in energy or my capacity for work. My curiosity about the world was unchanged, I still wanted to read, travel, learn. I had yet to visit Ravenna, Alsace, Bulgaria.

But the problems with my heart made me stop and think. Mom wasn't very old when she died, and the idea that my own life might not be any longer than hers, or even shorter, was grotesque, inconceivable.

Perhaps that was the first time I actually realized that I was going to die.

It is possible that I became bitter. It is possible that this might have been avoidable if I'd had greater elbow room within my soul, but I didn't. It was as if everything came together: my deteriorating health, a sense that I was losing the influence I once had, that I was increasingly regarded as irrelevant, an old man with anachronistic values, while at the same time literature was getting lost in contemporary society.

It was a depressing period for those who thought that literature was something major, something important and everlasting, something that deserved a great deal better than both its contemporary practitioners and its critics. The same could be said of the seventies, but it didn't seem so noticeable then. In those days the majority of my work was focused on the classics, and I was intoxicated with the knowledge that I had been granted access to a world I had only dreamed of in the past. Plus I was younger and maybe I found it easier to adapt, to overlook things that I now found difficult to deal with.

Literature had become a political cudgel again, but I felt as if it were different this time, as if it lacked a kind of jauntiness that used to be there, maybe even a kind of joy. These days its main aim seemed to be to highlight its practitioners' impeccable values, rather than achieving something good out of genuine concern for those on whose behalf it allegedly spoke. The whole thing became a drama. The cultural pages in the daily newspapers tainted whatever they touched, they tainted art with their eyes, literature with their reading. They would hold up a novel as an example of this or that, of good or evil. The critics delivered their verdicts as if they were engaged in a war where everything must be assigned to one side or the other, their own or the enemy's: This book doesn't suit our purpose, this one is dispensable, this one is undesirable.

I felt as if everything I had built up was falling apart right in front of me. It wasn't because I didn't understand contemporary life, I understood it very well. I understood profit maximization and clickbait, I understood ideological and opportunistic driving forces. I just didn't understand how they had managed to take everyone hostage.

If only there were something to give me hope, I often thought. And then you arrived at Rydéns.

I admit that I didn't really notice you at first. New interns showed up every season, most of them didn't make much of an impact. However, I preferred those to the other kind, the ones who had decided to be offensive and argumentative, to make as big an impression as possible during the few months at their disposal. You were quiet but looked intelligent, there was an alertness in your expression during all those meetings you sat in on. I thought you could probably have come out with far more interesting comments than many of the other windbags around the table if you hadn't had to interrupt them in order to get a word in edgewise.

And then your honesty took me by surprise. Jenny had pushed through yet another novel by a young woman about yet another young woman who drifted around Stockholm engaging in doomed relationships. I thought it was dreadful, written in a pseudo-lyrical style that felt intrinsically false. You saw it, and you dared to say so. I was both amused and impressed by the fact that you came to a major publishing house and described one of its new novels as contrived and dishonest. You didn't do so in order to draw attention to yourself, to make yourself appear interesting and contrary. You simply understood that it was a poor novel, just as you understood things that

I couldn't believe someone of your age would understand. I don't know what to call it, maybe an intuitive feeling for both literature and individuals, for the present and the past. You had realized that human nature was essentially the same deep down, that human impulses do not change.

I noticed that you were both an attentive reader and an attentive listener. Everyone can listen, as long as you can keep your mouth shut and manage to look more or less awake, but your listening was like an active part of the conversation, your comments were never superficial or trite.

It surprised me that a person with whom I felt such a bond was a young woman, from a completely different generation. We talked as if the age difference between us did not exist.

I gave the matter a great deal of thought before I invited you to the Opera Bar that first time. The memory of what had happened with Susanne still sent waves of shame coursing through my body. I was also afraid that things would go wrong for some reason, and would have a negative effect on our work at Rydéns. Then I thought, what the hell, life is too short to put off what you want to do. Admittedly I was married now, but the age difference between us made it all feel so innocent that I was certain Marianne would have been fine with the knowledge that we shared a bottle of wine occasionally.

In the end I never got around to telling her. I don't really know why. Maybe I wanted a part of my life that was purely mine, a place where I could be without having to report back to someone else. I wasn't a dishonest person, I knew that, but I suppose there was inevitably an element of excitement. An excitement that was kind of staged and not at all dramatic, but excitement nonetheless, and maybe I was the sort of person who appreciated exactly that type of excitement.

I think I can admit that there was excitement, and I think we were both in agreement that it existed. We couldn't mention it, we could barely even acknowledge it in our minds. It was abstract and nameless, but no less true because of that.

Provence—it sounded like a promise of paradise, but as usual I quickly grew bored. It felt wrong right from the start, I had been dragged into someone else's dream, once again I was forced to make someone else's life my own.

There were previous acquaintances everywhere, friends of Marianne's ex-husband, the successful lawyer. I wasn't exactly jealous, but I did experience a nagging sense of discomfort. I didn't like the fact that her friends in France knew things about her that I didn't know, that they were judging me with another man as a yardstick, a man who was very different from me in many ways, a man I hadn't particularly taken to on the few occasions when I had met him in passing.

They restrained themselves politely when old memories took up too much space in the conversation, but sometimes, especially after a few bottles of wine, they couldn't help it. Their need to recount anecdotes from the summer of 1991 was greater than their desire to make me feel comfortable, and occasionally one of them would smile at me with a mixture of sympathy and smugness, as if I were a child sitting at the table with the grown-ups while they talked about matters I didn't fully understand.

They were interested in me when they stood to gain from the transaction, when they were going to be able to pass on gossip with me as their source: What about Björn Holm, the famous crime writer published by Rydéns who had been in all the papers, suspected of drug offenses? They leaned forward across the table, their drunken, demanding gazes fixed on me.

I also grew tired of rosé wine very quickly, I felt as if it stuck to the inside of my mouth in an unpleasant way. Waking up in the morning after too much rosé was a particular torment, and it happened with increasing frequency because the wine provided me with armor against the socializing in the evenings.

Why didn't I get up and walk away? I sometimes wondered. Why didn't I pack my bags and leave? But where would I go? With hindsight my life before Marianne appeared to be a long, monotonous, straight road, like a highway. Admittedly it was lined with sparkling lights, but the sparkle was only ever on the surface, not something to build a life around. I wanted a context, and now I had a context. It might not have been the context I would have chosen if I had been able to choose, if I had been able to direct my own life somehow, but that is not possible, and what I had was better than nothing.

It wasn't a perfect life, but on the whole there were no serious issues. It was a life.

Instead I went out in the ridiculous little rental car and visited churches. The history was the only thing I really liked about France, and I secretly fantasized about leaving the South of France on my own, driving north to Chartres to see the cathedral then continuing on to Rouen or Amiens. I had only seen pictures of the cathedrals, but they rose up like huge mountains, as if some force of nature had intervened to help humanity create the most magnificent monuments imaginable to the glory of their god. I thought it must be cool inside, cool and peaceful.

Marianne preferred the small Matisse chapel in Vence. Compared to a Gothic cathedral it seemed banal, it put me in a bad mood. There was nothing astounding about it, just a few stained-glass windows with lurid colors and designs that looked like every other design but purported to be something special. Marianne really did think they were special, or at least she said so, and when she got into conversation with the guide, she came across as deeply affected by the place, she couldn't stop talking. That annoyed me too, the fact that she seized every opportunity to show off her French. I didn't speak French, languages have always been my weak point. My English is stilted at best, and apart from that I speak only Swedish. It was childish of me, but the whole situation, the feeling of being in enemy territory, meant that I had no desire whatsoever to learn any more French beyond the "*bonjour*" and "*merci*" that everyday life compelled me to use.

I read a biography of Ovid, he had been exiled to the Black Sea, to what is Romania today and was then the remotest outpost of the Roman Empire. "Here I am a barbarian, because no one understands what I say," he wrote, and I felt exactly the same. It was as if everything I knew, everything I was capable of, simply drained away when I was in France: my sense of humor, my education, my entire personality, all the things that someone else might have appreciated about me. Then I had to smile at my self-pity. Exiled to Provence, banished to a villa with four bathrooms and a pool.

I felt dumb and spoiled, we were all spoiled. Marianne with her ridiculously expensive sandals and her exaggerated joy in life, her sons, who had started showing up with girlfriends—equally unbearable, equally predictable with their blond hair and tasteless clothes, signaling nouveau riche upper-class Stockholm. And then there was me, getting older with each passing day, irritably discontented in such a beautiful place.

I thought about you more and more often. It was hard to contact you, and sometimes it was simply easier not to try, because then it was easier not to miss you. I decided to send you a postcard one summer, but when I sat down with it on the table in front of me, I didn't know what to write. All my words were simultaneously too big and too small. I think I put something a little too nondescript, but afterward I was both pleased and a bit embarrassed. It was only a postcard, but it felt like a grand romantic gesture, it excited me. It made me feel young. No doubt that sounds ridiculous.

I wondered what you were doing during those summer days and, I admit, those summer nights. I had realized that there was something going on between you and Richard, and I pictured the two of you hanging out together. Laughing, maybe going on vacation, making plans, plans that of course had nothing to do with me, plans for the future.

It was an ill-defined feeling of jealousy, if it could even be classified as jealousy. The idea that I should be in his shoes was literally unthinkable, unimaginable. And yet the thought of you and him evoked a dull, nagging distaste. I told myself that he was the problem, with his stupid book about weeds that he had steered in a direction that fit perfectly with the zeitgeist: There are in fact no weeds, it's just that people don't want certain plants in the places where they happen to have taken root. It was a thesis perfectly suited to articles in the press and discussions on morning TV, it gained traction both in Sweden and internationally, according to the many positive reviews it could make us more tolerant and teach us to see beauty in the humble and insignificant.

This was an appealing hypothesis, of course, and it wasn't Richard who dictated the mood of the moment, he simply wanted to profit from it, just like everyone who had something to sell. And to be honest I knew I would have had a problem with whoever you had met.

I enjoyed working with you, even though I had stopped finding the job itself especially enjoyable a long time ago.

I liked to have you sitting there in the armchair in my office, I liked looking at you when you were absorbed in whatever we were working on, concentrating hard, your face lit by the blue glow of the computer screen. Every time I had to leave—because it was always me who had to leave sooner or later, always me who had something else waiting—it felt like bursting a bubble, destroying something beautiful and delicate, a place where I would have preferred to stay.

The fact that I cared about what was happening at Rydéns more than anything, yet at the same time I didn't care much at all, must have seemed both strange and contradictory. That was what happened, that was the position I found myself in. I had given such a large part of my life to doing something I believed in, and I didn't want to admit that I had stopped believing in it. I might as well be honest now: Many of the titles I published under the Andromeda imprint weren't particularly good.

In the beginning I thought they were, I was intoxicated by doing something new and successful. However, as the years passed it became increasingly difficult to find something that fit. Those who had been young and exciting became part of the establishment, and no new voices came along to fill the gap. In spite of this the imprint still had an excellent reputation, we almost always secured interviews in advance and reviews on the day of publication. I had managed to persuade the entire literary world that Andromeda really did have something better to offer.

I knew you felt the same. You still believed in literature, just as I had when I was younger. Positive reviews
and flattering prize nominations made you happy. I found
this touching, and I wanted to protect you from turning
into a cynic like me, I wanted you to grow into one of
those who burned. Who became fire.

And yet I would have liked to point out how strange
it is that we are so rigidly defined by our occupation, that
we put so much time and energy into our work, when in
fact it is so unimportant in the end. I was lucky, I had been
at the center of events during an era that many people
would have loved to experience. I had stood on the roof
terrace at Rydéns for so many spring parties and watched
the sun go down over Stockholm's silhouette, over the
church spires and the copper rooftops with their beautiful
patina. I had stood there with generation after generation
of leading authors, handed them a glass of wine and said,
"You see those coasters? They've been in use since the
very first parties at Rydéns. One was even found among
Strindberg's effects after his death."

I made up that story at a party shortly after I joined
Rydéns, I just came out with it, and then it acquired a
life of its own. It didn't occur to anyone to question such
a good anecdote. Anyone who could have done so was
gone, and the new staff willingly drank it in. I even found
it in a book that was written to celebrate Rydéns's cen-
tenary, it had become a part of the publishing house's
history. No one, not even a Strindberg expert, ever in-
vestigated the story, because everyone wanted it to be

true. It became my quiet obituary, in a way my most successful narrative.

It is easy to believe that romantic love is the high point of life. I once thought so too. That's what came across in the books I read. However, few of the most memorable moments of my life have played out within the frame of romantic love, few of the real encounters with another person. Sometimes it has seemed to me that love almost has the opposite effect. As soon as you have conquered someone, or allowed yourself to be conquered, and gotten used to the situation, a situation without any uncertainty, a situation where everything is out in the open, then the desire to let someone further in disappears, to dig deeper within yourself for the sake of another person, to dig deeper into her. It then becomes easier to stay on exactly the same level, no one wants to hear about new darkness or perversions from someone with whom you have a joint mortgage. That kind of thing is reserved for the time before, the time when you are still in a negotiation phase.

That is probably why new people are so tempting, not necessarily for their own sake but for yours. The new and the fleeting offer a chance for you yourself to become new. A chance to be seen as you want to be seen, maybe as the person you really are: a fragment that contains more truth than the whole.

Obviously that's what I was thinking during those afternoons in Bakfickan at the Opera Bar. That we came into existence in each other's eyes, that we became the people we both wanted to be. It also felt as if we saw each other for the individuals we really were—paradoxically, because we both saw a reflection of ourselves in the other. And for the first time in forever I felt alive. That made me both happy and sad: happy to have found someone who wanted to listen to what I had to say, and sad to realize that this had been missing throughout my life. Someone who actually wanted what I had to give. There was so much that was important to me, and it struck me that I had never shared it with anyone. You liked hearing about what I had read and what it meant to me, you wanted to hear about the things that had shaped me throughout my life. You preferred those confidences to the tales I had gotten used to telling, the anecdotes about famous authors and Nobel Prize winners that everyone usually wanted to hear. It was as if the world became new to me when I had the chance to tell you about it, as if I became a new person in my own eyes.

I began to look forward to our Thursdays in a way I hadn't looked forward to anything for a very long time. I often paid a little more attention to what I wore on those days.

"You're looking very stylish today," Marianne commented one Thursday morning when I was standing in front of the bedroom mirror knotting my tie. "Is there something special happening?"

"Board meeting," I mumbled.

It wasn't a lie, nor was it the whole truth. I had a board meeting in the morning, but I had chosen the tie because of you.

I might have been pathetic, but it never felt that way. With you nothing ever felt anything but pure and clean, all feelings clear and uncomplicated. I never found it problematic to celebrate with you when decisions you had made worked out well; it was obvious that you were talented. I was proud of you and happy to feel that way.

Do you remember my birthday party? You stood there on the lawn, looking a little bit lost among the other guests. If I had been a different kind of person I would have put my arm around your shoulders and introduced you to everyone, told them you were the one who would eventually take over from me. I was proud to see so much good in you, and to glimpse a reflection of myself in that quality. It was an affirmation I had never fully experienced before, and it was remarkably satisfying. Maybe that had also been missing from my life.

When I got sick my life revolved around sitting at this desk, in this house, far away from both you and the city in every way. When I did catch the train into town, I suddenly felt like a stranger. I had no place or function, like a transplanted organ that the body tries to reject: I no longer fit in. To be fair, most of my trips involved sitting in waiting rooms. I spent many hours in rooms with dog-eared magazines and the obligatory potted plants, a limbo, both aesthetically and existentially. It was almost worse than the actual appointments with doctors. It's not good for one's self-image to be a person who spends a lot of time sitting in waiting rooms.

I was afraid that you would begin to see me as I had begun to see myself. That the sense that we were alike would disappear, that the age difference would finally create a barrier between us. I didn't want to be someone you told to go carefully on icy sidewalks, someone you thought of as old and decrepit, one day maybe outdated, irrelevant. Someone you saw because you felt sorry for him.

I know that's what happened, and I also know that I pushed our relationship in that direction. It's funny, because it's a common theme in literature, one of those archaic structures we used to discuss: fearing something so much that you unconsciously bring it about. Like King Oedipus. And yet I let it happen in my own life. I became someone else in your eyes, and I had only myself to blame. In a way it had to do with my illness, because few situations are as infinitely lonely as being at the mercy of your body. It was an experience I couldn't share with you, and I had grown accustomed to being able to share things with you.

I started to drink more, even though I should have been drinking less. I became self-pitying and probably not very nice. It's a depressing thought, to become someone you don't want to be. But perhaps I wanted to push you away in order to save both of us: me from the feeling of being abandoned, you from having to feel sorry for me. It somehow felt simpler if you didn't want to see me, didn't even want to answer my calls.

Needless to say, it was a stupid strategy. There was still so much I wanted to tell you. It is a great asset to believe that you don't deserve anything special—I began to understand that as I grew older, and I could see you were the same. How many conversations have I had with people who never asked anything from me in return? All those authors I worked with and found out so much about. I knew about their illnesses and divorces, their financial problems and their broken family relationships. I listened to them and then I read their books on the same subjects. They rarely asked me questions. "How was your summer?" they might wonder, but no one found out that my mom had died, and it would never have occurred to any of them to ask.

I liked the fact that you were so similar to me. And I liked the fact that it was for the same reasons: We had both come from nothing special, hoping for something better but never expecting it. I think it is an attitude you have to be born into, just as you are born into the opposite stance—knowing with complete confidence that the world belongs to you. That was what I dreamed of when I was young, but those dreams carry the risk of being disappointed. You start searching for openings everywhere, openings that will take you forward, toward what you believe you deserve. That makes it hard to live honestly. One of the many things we have in common is that we value honesty above everything.

I guess that's why I am writing this. As an attempt to be honest with you to the end. Because there was so much I never said to you, even though we talked so much. And so many things we never did, although I don't really know how we could have done them. There was no framework, no prescriptive rules as there are for every other kind of relationship. But we should probably have seen each other more often. We should have talked even more. It is idiotic to have someone in your life with whom everything feels so self-evident, yet not take care of that relationship in every possible way. I know you would have wanted the same, but it was even harder for you to steer things in that direction.

Sometimes my thoughts drifted off in unacceptable ways, brushing against the idea of being with you in those unassuming hours that make up the majority of our lives. I pictured us standing side by side in a kitchen preparing dinner, sitting side by side on a sofa, traveling together. I wondered what it would have been like to have you with me in France, in the passenger seat of a rented car on the way to visit the cathedral in Chartres. I still haven't seen the cathedral in Chartres.

I am getting sentimental now, there is no point in pretending I'm not. It often happens when I think of you.

Do you remember you once told me that you felt as if you had spent your whole life running? I understood exactly what you meant, I had done the same. I had run alone, just as you had. But during those years it felt as if we were running together.

It felt as if we were running toward home.

The epigraph on page v is a version of a quotation from Novalis, *Heinrich von Ofterdingen* (Berlin, 1802).

The quotations on pages 28 and 162 are from the Swedish edition of Sappho, *Poems and Fragments*, translated by Vasilis Papageorgiou and Magnus William-Olsson (Stockholm: FIB:s Lyrikklubb, 1999); translated from the Swedish by Marlaine Delargy.

The quotation on page 124 is from Vilhelm Ekelund, *Båge och Lyra* (Framtiden, 1912); translated from the Swedish by Marlaine Delargy.

The quotation on page 131 is from Rainer Maria Rilke's poem "Archaïscher Torso Apollos" [Archaic Torso of Apollo], *Neuen Gedichte* (1908); translated from the German by Marlaine Delargy.

The quotation on page 171 is from Ovid, *Tristia. Ex Ponto*; translated from the Swedish by Marlaine Delargy.

ABOUT THE AUTHOR

THERESE BOHMAN grew up outside of Norrköping and now lives in Stockholm. Her debut novel, *Drowned*, received critical acclaim both in Sweden and internationally, and was selected as an Oprah Winfrey Summer Read. Her second novel, *The Other Woman* (Other Press, 2014), was short-listed for the Nordic Council Prize and Swedish Radio's Fiction Prize, while her third novel, *Eventide* (Other Press, 2016), was short-listed for Sweden's most prestigious literary award, the August Prize. Bohman is an arts journalist who regularly contributes to one of Sweden's largest newspapers, *Expressen*, and to the magazine *Tidningen Vi*.

ABOUT THE TRANSLATOR

MARLAINE DELARGY studied Swedish and German at the University of Wales, Aberystwyth, and she taught German for almost twenty years. She has translated novels by many authors, including Kristina Ohlsson; Helene Tursten; John Ajvide Lindqvist; Theodor Kallifatides; Johan Theorin, with whom she won the Crime Writers' Association International Dagger in 2010; and Henning Mankell, with whom she won the Crime Writers' Association International Dagger in 2018. Marlaine has also translated nine books in Viveca Sten's Sandhamn Murders series and two books in her Åre Murders series.